Harmony,

Enjoy the

been Cleared for Time Travel!

Love,

Shane Bryan 9/30/23

MW00526500

Cleared for Time Travel

Shane Bryan

BookLocker
Trenton, Georgia

Published by BookLocker.com, Inc., Trenton, Georgia.

Printed on acid-free paper.

BookLocker.com, Inc.
2023

First Edition

DEDICATION

For Mom, Granny, and GAL,
thank you for the tremendous support through any turbulence on this
flight through life.

CHAPTER ONE

The sunlight shines through broken clouds, providing a spotlight that illuminates the land below my tires. Waves cresting on the ocean are given a grand illuminance by the sun's rays. Trees on the opposite side of the boardwalk whistle and sway as the breeze rolls off the crashing waves and up the sandy beach.

I could not think of a better summer day for a bicycle ride along the Atlantic Ocean. The salt air lands gently on my cheeks as wave after wave engulfs the beach's edge. I'm relieved to have a day off from adding legal documents to a computer server. I love my job, but some days it can be tiresome. This beach cruiser seems to pedal itself along the boardwalk as I head to my favorite spot for a late breakfast.

The Bluefin Café is bustling with locals sipping hot coffee, chewing over the latest gossip, and enjoying their breakfast. Located in the tree branches above, the birds sing a cheery tune, fluttering around the doorway as guests step in and out of the restaurant. Each bird is hoping for a scrap treat left behind by a departing guest. I hop off my purple beach cruiser and prop it up with the kickstand, making sure to grab my plum-colored leather crossbody from the front basket.

I walk up the weather-beaten steps while my dirty blonde curls sway in the wind. "Bluefin Café" stands out in bold teal and cream colors on the painted glass, accompanied by a sand dollar that shows the restaurant's opening hours. Once I close the door behind me, numerous familiar voices sound in my ears.

I wave to Rita, who is sitting at a table near the forward entrance. Rita owns the Grandview Clothing Company — although we mostly still call it Rita's place — in the town square and is wearing her pink embroidered smock with her name on it.

Walking across the threshold, I stop at her table.

"Hi Rita!" I say. "I just had to stop and tell you that I loved your window display from the Fourth of July festivities. The fireworks were almost as beautiful as your window display."

"Hello, honey!" Rita says. "Really? You liked it? I threw it together so fast." Rita has always downplayed her true talent. Many designer stores in the big city would hire her if they saw her work.

"Yes! Your hard work inspires so many of us who walk by your shop. You brought the spirit of patriotism to life with the American flag and LED Christmas light fir works. How your nephew, Ivan, made the individual light strands burst in sequential order made the windows pop, especially at nighttime."

She blushes with enjoyment, and she continues eating her blueberry pancakes. I navigate across the aisle, finding that my favorite seafoam-colored booth is unoccupied. This specific seat enjoys a perfect view of the street, the boardwalk, and the beach beyond.

I set my belongings down and gaze through the large window, watching a baker's dozen catch the surf before the rush of tourists clogs up the water and the corresponding beach. There aren't as many locals enjoying the beach today since it's a little chilly this morning, but by this afternoon, our quaint beach will be turned into a colorful mosaic of umbrellas and beach towels.

The aroma of fresh-brewed coffee brings me back to the present. Turning, I can see the cooks' flipping pancakes behind the counter and dancing around the stovetops and fryers with their music. Moments later, I am overcome by a familiar, cloying perfume as Ruby, the café owner, approaches me. An older woman in a promiscuous red cocktail dress, her auburn hair is teased in a French twist coated with enough hairspray to light a small wildfire.

"Jackie, can I rustle you a cup of fresh coffee?" Ruby towers above me in her red pumps, brandishing a steaming jug.

"Coffee? Yes, I'd love some." I hand Ruby my pale blue cup, and she fills it to the brim.

"You want your usual, honey?" she asks, placing the now-full cup in front of me. Ruby never writes down her orders. Her memory is outstanding, and she sends everything to the kitchen using the electronic point of sale system.

I nod.

"Sure thing," she replies, as she smiles and strolls away to place the order. I reach over and take three of my favorite flavored mini creamer cartridges from the bowl on the tabletop — pumpkin spice creamer. She's always treated me like I'm her favorite niece, even though I'm just another regular in her café.

Sipping the delicious coffee, I think back to when Ruby bought this place in 1985, and how she quickly became a staple in Bluefin Cove, our little town in Maine. After the purchase was complete, the previous owners retired to Florida. Come to think of it, I just got a postcard in the mail last week from Alice and Henry, bragging about the sunshine and year-round fun.

Ruby brought many of her great-grandmother's recipes to the café, like sweet and sour cinnamon rolls and lobster benedicts with crispy bacon accompanied by a generous scoop of red potatoes. Many more of her recipes have landed on the signature menu.

Her grandson, Harrison, has worked in the café since he was 16, starting as a busboy and quickly working his way up to assistant manager. When Ruby leaves for her vacation at least four times a year, Harrison is in charge of the restaurant operations. She told me a while back that he will assume ownership when she decides to retire, as she couldn't be more pleased with his hard work and dedication.

I always start my morning late — and already it's nearly noon — with coffee and reading the news on my iPad. Sure, I have coffee at home, but today I feel like treating myself to some down-home Yankee hospitality and the chance to run into some of my neighbors.

Above the back counter, there's a 32-inch television that constantly plays the great TV shows of the past. Ruby has the TV set on a classic rerun network, 24/7. Even when the café is closed, I can see the TV playing in the dark through the large, unblinded windows.

Still drinking my coffee gradually, I hear someone call my name in a rich Kentucky accent. I turn my head and it's my dear friend Laurie Webb. Laurie works at the Heavenly Waves Nursing home as the lead nurse. The guests at the home truly love her kind heart and funky attitude.

"Jackie, I just saw you here and had to drop by," she says, leaning in for quick and genuine hug. "What are you doing here all by your lonesome?"

"It's so good to see you." I gush. "Have you hired a new activities director yet?" The last person retired a few weeks ago, and Laurie has been filling in before her shift for an hour just to give the residents a bingo or trivia challenge. The winner gets a quarter, and that will buy them a soda from the vending machine.

"No, not yet. I have to make sure that the person is qualified and really cares about the residents." Laurie declares. "I do have an interview next week." While Laurie is a tough woman, she cares about her patients with true compassion. "I have to run. You enjoy your brunch and I'll see you around." She leaves me to sip my coffee.

For the next few minutes, I sip my coffee and read an article in the *Bluefin Journal* about the new library being constructed in the heart of the town square. Then the television stops mid-program and starts playing a breaking news alert about some plane crash that's been found. But of course, they only give enough details to catch your attention.

I start looking around the bustling restaurant for Ruby or one of her staff. I see Ruby peer out from the kitchen, and I raise my hand to grab her attention. She hustles over.

"What is it, dear?" she asks, concerned.

"Oh, Ruby, could you please turn up the volume? I am trying to hear it."

She nods and navigates herself over to the counter. Pulling the remote from a drawer, she clicks the volume button a few times so the sound grows louder.

"That good?"

I nod, and Ruby returns to entering orders in the computer and pouring out fresh coffee. I wait for the stupid commercial to finish while gripping my half-empty cup. Finally, the news starts, and I sit frozen, staring up at the television.

The breaking news bulletin plays again, and the camera pans over the news anchors, along with the show's theme song. I tap my fingers on the table, irritated with the delay. Then the camera zooms in on a female reporter, her dark curly hair cut in a sophisticated bob. Her bright red lipstick is jarring against her pale skin.

"This is a breaking news story," she says. "Thank you for joining us today. I'm Robin Reynolds. Over fifty years ago, the world was stunned when a brand new, state-of-the-art jetliner disappeared over the Atlantic Ocean shortly after takeoff. Rescuers searched for weeks after the disappearance, but all passengers and crew were presumed lost at sea within a few days after the plane disappeared from coastal radar." The café is silent now, the other diners all glued to the broadcast.

The reporter is still speaking, but the video switches to an aerial view of a ship at sea.

"Well, that all changed today when the Navy Research Vessel, United States Ship Lavon, found the wreckage site while researching underwater sea life. We'll be back with more in just a moment."

The news switches to a commercial. Ruby walks over, places the steaming coffee carafe on the table before slipping into the booth across from me.

"Jackie," she murmurs discreetly. "That wasn't your dad's airplane, was it? The story sounds awfully familiar."

I purse my lips, trying to decide whether it's just a strong coincidence, or if my life is about to change.

"I'm not sure; the reporter didn't say what airline it was. Do you think it could be a coincidence?"

But before she can answer, the news anchor's intro starts up again.

"Oh! Wait, they're back, let's watch."

We both turn our attention back to the TV set. By this time, the customers are all chattering away again. Bluefin Cove is a small town, and when something from the past is dug up, the locals get excited. I can only imagine the fuel that this will add to the beauty parlor.

We both try to hear what the reporter is saying, but it's difficult to make out her words, even after Ruby raises the volume.

"Folks, keep it down," she finally hollers. "We're trying to hear the TV, please!" Everyone hushes as the anchor continues her report.

"In 1971, Americonic International Airways Flight Number 329 took off from John F. Kennedy International airport, destined for Rome. Twenty-five minutes into the flight, air traffic control lost all contact with the aircraft and its crew. The Canadian Coast Guard was dispatched shortly after to investigate the aircraft's last known coordinates. This morning, the underwater robot, *Sea Flyer*, was searching the ocean floor about 150 miles south of Nova Scotia and came across a debris field. After assessing the area and determining it was safe to proceed, the navigators spotted remnants of an airplane, including wings, tail, engines and other debris. It was not until the submersible came around the other side of the tail fin that they discovered the registration number, N723AI, painted on the fuselage."

The news anchor's voice continues to play, as the screen shows pictures of the aircraft before its disappearance.

"The Boeing 707 intercontinental jetliner was registered to Americonic International Airways. Along with the registration number, investigators were also given videos and picture evidence from the discovery. Upon reviewing the evidence, they saw the unique red, white and blue stars painted on what was left of the horizontal stabilizer. The USS Lavon team is working to salvage the wreckage from the seafloor and take it to a secure hangar. This is a developing news story, and we will bring you more details as they become available."

The channel flicks back to a 1970s show about big stars cruising the ocean on a lovely cruise ship. I turn to Ruby in shock.

"That was his airplane! My father's, I mean. That's it!"

Before Ruby can gather her thoughts for a response, my cell phone vibrates in my purse, one alert after another. Retrieving the phone, I see numerous texts from my little sister, Candice. Then my phone rings before I can read the messages.

"Hey, sis, did you —"

But she cuts me off. Candice shouts so loud I have to hold the phone away from my ear.

"SIS! Did you see the news? They found Daddy's airplane! Where are you? Are you home?"

Candice and I are the only family we have left. Mom and Dad were only children, and our grandparents died years ago. So, when big news happens in her life, she calls me right away as she knows I will guard her deepest secrets.

"I just saw it," I told her. "I'm at Ruby's."

"I'm closing up the shop for the rest of the day and heading to the house — I'll see you there!" There's a click as she hangs up. I lower my phone.

"I better head home, Ruby. If I pedal fast enough, I should be there by the time Candice is." I take a twenty-dollar bill from my purse and try to hand it over to Ruby. She denies my gesture and pats my hand.

"Oh, honey, it's on the house. You better get on your way."

I sling my plum purse over my shoulder and give Ruby a hug and a kiss on the cheek. Heading for the exit, I wave to a few people in the café who see me making the dash out. I trot down the creaking front steps to my bicycle.

My house is just ten minutes away. After tossing my purse in the basket, I start pedaling away from the café, then through the town square where our local farmers market is still in full swing. Of course, I need items from there, but I have no time to stop.

I ride along the shoreline, filling my lungs with fresh ocean air. I pass a few beachgoers, tourists and many pop-up shops. Bluefin Cove is a friendly community, where everyone knows each other's secrets. Just as I shake my head, thinking about all the town gossip that's swept through our little town through the years, I see Michelle.

She waves, and shouts from a small distance. "Where are you riding so fast?"

Faced with the time crunch, I slow down but do not stop fully.

"Hi! I've got to meet Candice at the house," I shout back and give a wave while holding the handlebar with one hand. She waves back and smiles and we lock eyes for only a second and I continue on.

I ride past a series of massive eastern white pine trees that line the sidewalks. Each of them stands sentinel before a front yard. Tim and Michael, our neighbors, are conversing on their front porch from their rocking chairs.

"Whoa, speed racer. Why are you hurrying? Is someone chasing you?" Tim asks while Michael sips on a mug that contains tea with a shot of vodka. Tim and Michael moved here a year ago after they retired from the crazy life of being a flight attendants for Southwestern International Airlines.

A few weeks back, Candice and I had dinner at their home for their tenth wedding anniversary. Michael cooked the most delicious steak that I have ever tasted, and Tim bought a French silk pie from the local baker in town.

"I'm meeting Candice!" I shout from the street, turning into my driveway. Not a moment later, I see Candice's Buick pull in behind me. Mom passed away a few years ago, and since I don't drive, she left the old Buick to my sister in her will. The motor turns off, and Candice steps out of the car. I lean my bike up against the house and swing my purse over my shoulder as I run to her.

"Can you believe they found it?" she blurts out, as I crush her in a sisterly hug. I turn towards Tim and Michael and wave. Candice waves as well and they return to their previous conversation.

"No," I tell her. "Not even a little bit. Come inside, though. We'll have tea and talk." Even though it's July, we still get a cool breeze in Maine — and hot tea is a great way to warm up and calm the nerves.

Candice unlocks the door — we've been living together ever since her husband was killed on the road during a winter storm back in 1999. He was a truck driver for 3B Trucking out of Portland, Maine. I follow Candice in and close the door behind me, and we both hang our purses on the coat rack and head for the kitchen.

The kitchen is filled with many memories. White lace embroidered curtains hang in the windows, the cabinets are a rich mahogany, and there's white quartz countertops Candice and I had installed just last month.

The Craftsman-style house was built in 1951 by the town's mayor. When he passed in 1972, Mom found the property in a real-estate advertisement and bought it the same day via the phone number posted within the ad. She decided to keep the original details, including the expensive wood trim, fixtures, appliances and even some of the furniture.

I snatch the white tea kettle from the drying rack by the white porcelain farm sink and begin to fill it. After the water reaches the top, I step over to the stove.

Our old gas stove is older than the house itself, but it has never failed me yet. Turning the dial to open the gas, I strike a match and light the burner, and the water begins to heat up.

Meanwhile, Candice is looking through her phone, reading the news stories about the recovery of the wreckage. I grab two teacups from the tea cabinet, the sugar caddy and the Christmas cookie tin we use for fresh tea bags and place them all on the table.

I walk back through the entryway, retrieve my iPad from my purse, and return to the kitchen table to lay it down next to the teacup. A few moments later, the tea kettle whistles. I bring it to the table and fill both our cups with hot water.

After returning the kettle to the range, I take my seat, crossing my legs under the table. Candice grabs a tea bag out of the tin and places it in the hot water. She hands me my favorite flavor, English Elegance.

After I fix my cup, I open the tablet case and start researching the news for any new information. I navigate to the search window, and a variety of news stories pop up, but none of them say anything different from what I've already heard at the café.

One story catches my eye. There's a picture of an aircraft called Majestic Eagle. There's a link below the photo, and I hurry to click it. A website opens a different window that displays a video. Pressing play, I hear a voice I haven't heard in years.

It's a female voice, bitter with emotion. "We are very sorry to inform you that Americonic International Airways has been notified by Navy personnel that the search and rescue has been discontinued indefinitely.

For further information, please contact the Americonic International Airways family care team."

The last time I heard that recording, and that same haunting voice, was when Candice and I were cleaning Mom's mess of a room when she passed away. She'd saved the recording on a mini cassette player.

"Was that the recording from Mom's cassette?" Candice asks me from across the table. I nod, continuing to read the story. The point of this specific article is to shine light on why the Navy called off the search so quickly.

I finish the article and turn to Candice. "You finding anything?"

She puts down her tea. "Nope, not yet. They all have same thing about the USS Lavon finding the wreckage, but nothing else."

I keep refreshing the screen, hoping a new story will develop — but no luck. After about an hour of us both scavenging the internet, I get up to turn on the kitchen television. It's been about an hour and a half since the news story broke, and maybe there's an update.

"Where's the dang remote?"

I rummage in the drawer under the counter, finally locating it. The TV is an old one, and it takes a few moments for the dinosaur to come alive.

The moment it powers up, I flip to the news channel and luckily, we're just in time. The story is about halfway through.

"The wreckage of Americonic Flight 329 will be housed in a hangar at the air base in Nova Scotia for the duration of the investigation. The wreckage will be under control of the National Transportation Safety Board, since the aircraft is American made and operated by a formerly US-based airline."

Candice frowns in thought. "What do you think are the chances that we could go there and see the wreckage?"

I consider it. "Oh, my, I'm not sure. Probably very slim, I'd imagine".

A few moments of silence follow. I'm trying to figure out who I would even call to ask about the wreckage or the newly reopened investigation.

Candice breaks my train of thought. "I remember Mom's stories about Dad leaving that day. She would go on about how handsome he looked in his freshly pressed uniform. I wish we could have known him better."

Tears are forming in her eyes. "How did Mom ever raise us on her own? The airplane disappeared on August 21, 1971. She had two young kids. I was a little over six months old, and Jackie, you were one and a half, right?"

I nod. "Yes. Well, the airline was very good to her, for one thing. She kept getting paychecks every week until the airline went bankrupt in 2002 after 9/11." I sit back down at the table. "Then there's the cans we collected, and we sold eggs for a while, right? It's incredible to see where we are now. I'm a data entry specialist at a law firm, and you have your own flower shop. Dad would be so proud of us."

Candice shakes her head. "But why did the airline go belly up? They were at the top of their game for so many years, even after the disappearance of dad's plane."

I look at the ceiling for a moment, collecting my thoughts.

"There were a bunch of terrible accidents after Flight 329. I think they had one every couple of years, then the recession just made things worse. Eventually, the CEO went on national TV in a televised hearing and declared they had no more funds to keep the operation going."

Candice continues typing on her phone, then holds it up for me to see. A video from 2002 begins to play.

"The airline that helped pioneer commercial aviation routes for more than seventy years is grounded tonight," the voiceover says. "As of today, Americonic has gone out of business." I remember seeing that on live TV when a news outlet did a special report on the airline.

We both turn back to our search engines. But there's very little about the disappearance of Flight 329. Even the public-access portal to the NTSB has very few details in its report.

I hold up my iPad for Candice. "Does it strike you odd that the NTSB only investigated for a few weeks after the disappearance and then closed the case? According to their website, there was a preliminary report that only has a short summary of the disappearance — and that's it."

"What does it say?" Candice asks. "Can you read it to me while I get a refill?"

I start reading. "On August 21, 1971, about 7:02 PM Eastern Standard Time, a Boeing 707-320B airplane, N723AI, disappeared from Boston center radar. After numerous Air Traffic Control contact requests, the controller, Bob Charlotte, contacted emergency services. The Canadian Coast Guard in Dartmouth rushed to the last known coordinates, 42 degrees north and 62 degrees west. No wreckage and/or debris were discovered at the last known coordinates. The aircraft was operated under the provisions of the Title 14 code of Federal Regulations, Part 91. The Boeing 707-320B operated under the airline Americonic International Airways and was operating route 329, John F. Kennedy International Airport enroute to Rome Fiumicino Leonardo da Vinci Airport. The aircraft was a newer model, having been put into service on May 20, 1971. According to Boston center Air Traffic Control, the pilots acknowledged that they were ascending to their cruising altitude of 35,000 feet. No further communications were recorded until the Air Traffic Control, Bob Charlotte, requested contact. The recorded Air Traffic Control communications were retained in a secure lab for further examination."

I put down my iPad. "That's it. There's nothing else in the report."

Candice looks confused. "All that information we already know. The news and conspiracy theorists spouted that for years after the incident. Is there anything else online about the disappearance?"

I shake my head. "No, that's it. The file states they closed the case on September 24, 1971." I finish my now-lukewarm tea. "Hey, let's order some food now, so it will be here by dinnertime. What sounds good? Chinese?"

"Sounds good to me! My usual, please. You want some money?"

"That's all right, I got it this time." I head into the entryway to get my debit card from my purse, then walk to the yellow wall phone in the kitchen. The landline is only there for our internet, but we house business cards on the holder below it. I pick up the business card for Harbor Noodle Company, the only Chinese restaurant in our little town.

As I reach for my cell phone, the screen lights up as it begins to ring. The caller ID pops up and says *US Government* under the phone number. The area code is not local.

"202? That's Washington, isn't it?" I express, looking over at Candice and pointing at the caller ID.

Candice gives me a warning look. "That must be a scam. Why would they be calling *us*?"

We let it go for a while, but then the phone stops ringing. I wait for a voicemail to come through on the machine, but there's just a click. Whoever it was must have hung up when the recording started.

"Scammer," I repeat. "I'm sure you're right."

Before I can say another word, the phone starts to ring again. And again, the caller ID displays *US Government.*

"What *now*?" Candice sighs. We hardly ever receive calls during the week, so this must be something important. Most of our friend's text, and my boss only chats within the office messaging app.

"Should I answer it? Scammers don't call twice in a row, do they?"

Candice vehemently shakes her head, but I can't resist.

I take a deep breath, then slide the green button to answer. Holding the receiver to my ear, I listen for a few seconds in silence.

A deep male voice says, "Miss Jette, this is Agent Taylor, Badge Number 5102153411 from the United States Air Force Aviation, Research and Discovery department in Washington, DC. I need to ask you a few questions. Is this a good time?"

My eyes grow wide and my heart pounds against my rib cage. I turn to Candice, and she must see my shocked expression, because she puts her hand to her mouth covering it slightly.

Agent Taylor speaks again without changing his tone. "Miss Jette, this is rather urgent. Do you have a moment? If your sister is there, please ask her to wait outside your home on the porch."

"Why does she need to wait on the porch?" I ask, then catch myself. "How did you know that we *have* a porch?" I motion furiously at the window, trying to indicate to Candice that she should look outside for unmarked sedans, like in the movies.

"Agent Taylor," I repeat, "how did you know about our porch?"

"Our records indicate that the house at 1241 Oldham Avenue has a front porch with white rocking chairs, two to be exact, and a table with white carnations."

Now I'm *sure* it's a scammer.

"Mr. Taylor, I don't know what kind of game you're playing, but I'm hanging up now. Oh. And they're tiger lilies." Not giving him the chance to respond, I tap the phone's red button to end the call. I do miss the days where you could just slam the receiver on the wall as a statement of your frustration.

"Total fake," I shake my head at Candice. "Probably a news reporter trying to get the inside scoop from the captain's daughter."

Not even a moment later, my cellphone rings on the table.

Candice looks down at the screen. "Uh, Jackie? It's the government again."

I refuse to answer the phone, so she does instead. She puts it on speakerphone.

"Hello?" Candice asks, cautiously. Whoever he is, the man recognizes her voice.

"Hello, Candice, this is Agent Taylor. Would you please hand the phone back to Jackie? I can assure you that I am not with the press and that I am a real agent for the government."

Not believing him, I shout from across the room, "Prove it!"

There's a long pause.

"Okay, ladies, this should prove it." We move closer to the speaker, waiting. "When Paul Jette was declared deceased a few weeks after the disappearance, you mother received a check from the United States Government for an amount that provided enough money to move you all to Bluefin Cove."

"Pfff," I huff. "If you have that information, then you should be able to tell me the exact amount written on the check, I suppose."

"Sure. The amount on the check was $73,127.34 from the Treasury Department. Made out to your mother as 'Enlisted Services.'"

I feel that he knows I'm testing him. Leaving Agent Taylor on the line, I race down the hall to pull out Mom's bank books from the hallway hutch. I open up the ledger from her checking account. *$73,127.34.*

Agent Taylor is still on speakerphone. As I make my way back to the kitchen, I can hear his voice. "Oh, and I might add, Miss Jette, that it was cashed on December 7, 1971, at Apache Central Bank in New York."

I rush back to the table. "Hold, please," I splutter, as I push the hold button on my phone screen.

When I speak to Candice, my voice is shaking. "There are only three people in this world who know the truth, and mom is dead. How did he know the amount and date when Mom cashed that check?"

We stare at each other.

"No reporter would know that," Candice says. "I believe him."

I press hold again. "Okay, Agent Taylor. You have our attention now."

Agent Taylor clears his throat. "Candice, would you please let us have a moment?"

She looks at me and shakes her head, her face pale. "No," I say, as forcefully as I can muster. "Whatever you have to say, you can say it to both of us."

There's a pause, then the agent continues. "Jackie, what do you know about your dad's career with Americonic and the Pentagon?"

Stunned, I feel my jaw drop open. Staring at Candice, I reply, "Dad wasn't in the military. I know he flew special missions to Korea since the airline had chartered flights there. That's what the check was for." Mom never said anything about Dad being in the military or government beyond that. "This is news to us, Agent Taylor."

"Ladies, are you aware of the new information we have on your dad's missing plane?"

"Of course. We saw the news a few hours ago. That a Navy vessel found pieces of the plane, or something like that?"

"That's correct, ma'am. My team received word directly from the ship. Since the debris field is closer to Nova Scotia, the wreckage will be held there for the duration of the investigation."

"Mr. Taylor, what does any of this have to with us?" I can tell my cheeks are flushed, and I put my hands to my face. "Are you calling all the victims' families to notify them of this discovery?"

There's a long pause. I'm sure he's choosing his next words very carefully. For a while I wonder if he's hung up. Then he replies, "You are the only subject I am permitted to speak with."

Subject? What the heck? "Hold please," I tell him, and put the phone on mute again.

"This sounds bad," I say to Candice. "When did we turn into *subjects?"*

My sister looks down at the phone warily, like it's a scorpion getting ready to strike. "This..." she hesitates. "This could be bigger than we think."

I unmute the phone, and Agent Taylor immediately resumes talking. "Ladies, I feel that this would be better to discuss in person. I'll be in touch." He disconnects the call.

"Did he just hang up on us?" Candice gasps. "What the —"

"I don't know." I get up from the table again. "What I *do* know is, I'm starving. I couldn't eat anything today. Let's order food before it's too late." I finally place our order through the delivery app on my phone.

Once that's done, we move out to the front porch. I scan the area for any unsavory vehicles or unknown people on the sidewalk. After I feel the coast is clear, I take my seat next to Candice with the table between us. Leaning back in my white rocking chair, I muse, "What could Dad have done in the military? He was always too busy flying around the world."

"Well, exactly," Candice laughed. "He had the perfect cover. An Americonic pilot traveling around the world would fly right under the radar. I bet he was working with the CIA."

"No *way*. Like James Bond or something?" We both laugh at how ridiculous that sounds. "If I had to guess, he probably flew some important politician to a speech in Europe."

We talk until the food arrives, then bring it inside. Munching our way through our honey almond shrimp and sesame chicken with broccoli, we can't help but continue talking about our mysterious government "agent."

"Candice, what do you think he meant when he said that he only wants to speak with me?" I wonder out loud.

She shrugs, wiping some sauce from the corner of her mouth with a paper napkin. "You got me. I'm sure we'll find out tomorrow, and if not, we'll play hard to get and fish it out of him."

Once we're stuffed to the brim, we clean up the kitchen and move to the living room for a nightcap. The day has unleashed many questions, and my head is twirling. "Hey, you want to play a card game?" I ask, as I am sure that she is having the same motion in her mind.

"You're on!" Candice says and dashes to the card table in the den. "My fingers are feeling hot and in the groove. I hope you brought your A game." Removing the cards from the drawer, she stacks and shuffles them thoroughly.

The best part about playing cards is not the victory or the thrill of winning but the personal conversations between us. Candice has been so busy recently with her shop in town, and we haven't had any time for a card game in a while. Candice does have lucky hands tonight, as she beats me by nearly five thousand points.

Failing miserably to keep my eyes open, I decide to turn in for the night as does Candice. We check the door locks, close the window blinds and head upstairs to our rooms.

Melting into my soft Egyptian sheets, I check my tablet one more time before turning out the lights. There's a message from an unknown number. My heart starts to race a bit when I see the same 202 area code. It reads: *Hello Ms. Jette. This is Agent Taylor. I will be arriving tomorrow morning. I will let you know the time soon.*

I can't run to Candice's room fast enough. I throw on my housecoat, hurry across the hall, and bust the door open, not even bothering to knock. She's still watching television and before she can react to my dramatic entrance, I shout out, "He texted me!"

I read Agent Taylor's message out loud, but Candice looks confused. "Why is he making this long trip? And why so soon? Don't they have to plan things out far in advance?"

"I don't know," I admit. "You're right, the whole thing's weird."

Why does this stranger from the government want to meet us so urgently? Deciding not to worry about it, I set my alarm for 7 a.m. to make sure I wake up in time to get ready.

Returning to my bed, I close my eyes for the night.

CHAPTER TWO

I toss and turn a million times that night. Finally, my alarm sounds, and I roll out of my bed, wishing I'd had a few more hours of slumber. I sit up straight and feel diminished as my usual waking time is 11 a.m. or later. Given how unusual the plans are for today, this is a one-time exception.

Slipping into my housecoat, I creep down the wooden staircase. I raise the tab on the coffee pot, remove the old coffee pouch, and throw in a new one. While the coffee percolates and sputters, I peer out the kitchen window. It's a ghostly, foggy morning.

Sitting in my big chair in the living room, I sip the hot coffee and slowly return to my normally caffeinated state of well-being. The news reports on television are the same as yesterday, with no new information. Flipping through the usual channels, I land on our little town's local network. I nearly spit out my mouthful of coffee. There's a photo of my dad on the screen, with the caption, *Local residents' father was the captain of the ill-fated jetliner.*

The reporter narrates a little brief about how we moved here after his death, along with pictures from last year's community gala to raise money for the animal shelter. I was proud of that gala. That night, we raised $5,000 for food and medicine for the pups — and not a penny went into some greedy CEO's pocket.

The grandfather clock to my right begins to chime. 7:30 a.m. I hope Agent Taylor calls ahead to let us know when he'll be here.

"Morning," a zombified voice calls out from the bottom of the stairs. Candice waves and then heads for the coffee station. She grabs her coffee and joins me in the living room. As we wake up, we start talking about what Agent Taylor might be telling us today.

About twenty minutes later, both Candice and I dress nicely and put our hair up so we'll look somewhat professional when he arrives. The time is now 8 a.m., and we still haven't heard from Agent Taylor. Candice proposes we go have breakfast at Ruby's before he arrives. "After all," she coaxes, "we won't be eating for a few hours at least once he gets here. Who knows how long he'll want to talk to us?"

"Sure, let's go." After a quick drive in the Buick, we arrive at the café. Clearly, it's not very busy. Granted, most of the locals don't get here until 10 a.m. for the senior special: decaf coffee, low-cholesterol eggs and a free ticket to the bingo hall.

"Hello Candice, Jackie! Girls, what's new, what's hip?" Ruby greets us, while walking us to my favorite table. Candice and I just laugh, since we're not sure what to say. We take our seats, but Ruby's still waiting for an answer.

Just like my aunt Jess always says, it's better to hide in plain sight. "We have a meeting today with a man from out of town. He wants to give us some information about Dad." Ruby nods her head and goes over the usual café talk about specials.

I'm glad that she doesn't ask us anymore investigative questions in exchange for our bland response. If even she did, we don't have the answers to tell her.

Then suddenly, it registers. Ruby stops mid-sentence. "Oh! What have you learned about the crash? Anything new?" In the meantime, she fills our pale blue coffee mugs and awaits our response.

"Not really," I tell her. "We're still in the dark. And since Americonic closed its doors in 2002, I'm not sure if we'll *get* any more information." I don't mention Agent Taylor, though. Somehow, that seems like too big of a risk to take with so little information. Ruby is summoned to another table while we open the menu flap.

Reviewing the menu, we both decide that our usual selection will do and talk about the people strolling by on the boardwalk. There aren't many tourists out on this chilly morning, but the usual folks from the Heavenly Waves Nursing home are out walking to get their blood pumping before lunch is served in the nursing home dining room, Poseidon's Hideaway.

I don't think I've ever been here this early to witness the residents on their morning routine. If I have, it was years ago.

"Who's opening the shop today?" I ask my sister, sipping my coffee. Candice owns the only floral shop in town. She named it Finding Floral, which I thought was brilliant.

"I'll get Grace to do it. That big order's due in a few days, and we have it all done, pretty much. Just a few minor details." She puts her coffee down when Ruby returns, and we tell her we want our usuals, which consists of pumpkin cinnamon pancakes for me and Candice's "Two by Two by Two": two eggs, two slices of bacon and two buttermilk pancakes. We can hear the cooks moving around in the kitchen as they start to get busy.

"I bet the Bluefin Bowling League is going to love your arrangement." The League has a championship banquet every year around this time, and it's Candice's fifth year providing the floral arrangements. Last year, she won a prize from the mayor's office for best original design.

Ruby brings over two large, steaming plates, and we unroll our silverware and dig into the food. While we're still eating, a rather tall and well-built man approaches our table.

I look closer and notice that he has the brightest blue eyes that I have witnessed. The black-skinned gentlemen could not be a day over thirty, as he had not one wrinkle on his entire face or neck. The heathered blue blazer fit well over his broad shoulders, and his dark jeans did not underrepresent his muscular legs either.

"Candice, Jackie, it's so good to see you in person." When he speaks, I'm expecting him to have a high-pitched voice as he is so young. But, to our surprise, his voice is deep and masculine. We both stare for a moment, enjoying his voice.

Oh. It's him.

Agent Taylor takes a seat and orders a cup of coffee, though neither of us invited him.

I narrow my eyes and address him in a flat monotone. "Agent Taylor, nice to meet you and welcome to Bluefin Cove. You'll have to imagine us on a warmer day."

He smiles at my sarcasm and reaches into his coat pocket. Removing his credentials, he flips the little booklet open and shows it to me across the table and then to Candice to prove his identity, although I already knew it was him from the moment he spoke.

Once he replaces the ID, he leans casually back in the booth as though he owns the place. "I hope you both can forgive me for popping in here. I saw Candice's car in the front parking lot and thought that we could start with coffee." On cue, Ruby brings over his coffee, then rushes off to tend to other tables.

"How did you get here so fast? Isn't Washington like 500 miles away?" Candice asks before setting down her fork. "And how did you know it's my car?"

"I saw your motor vehicle records in your file. Not very many historic Buicks like yours on the road anymore."

Taken aback by his remark, I cannot help but think our so-called *file* has more information that just her motor vehicle records. And furthermore, why is that important enough to be in our file?

I jump in. "So, why do you have a file on Candice and me? Also, why do you need to know the make and model of her car?" The food's aroma rises to my nose, but with how uncomfortable I am with Agent Taylor's *file* on us, I can't bear to eat another bite.

"Well, I have both of your case files here in my briefcase. As for how I got here, I drove that government-issued black SUV sitting out front. I have orders to stay here until further notice from my boss." He picks up his coffee and takes a long gulp. "I have to interview you both today, and then I have no idea what I'm doing after."

"Do you want anything to eat?" I ask. The guys practically drained his coffee cup; he must be starving.

"No, I'll grab a bite later, after we finish. Would you all be okay if we started the interview right here?" He pulls out a notebook and pencil from the inside coat pocket of his blazer.

"Here?" Candice asks. "How stupid do you think we are? You must not be from a small town, Agent Taylor. This diner is Gossip Central Station."

I shrug. "We might as well. People will have no idea what we are talking about."

But Candice just shakes her head.

"Okay," I concede. "Well, why don't we meet you back at our house, Agent Taylor? I assume you already have the address tucked away with many more surprises in that Poppins designer briefcase?"

"Yes, I do. Let's meet in twenty — I need to check in at my hotel. I heard the Bluefin Oasis is like a Hawaiian resort or something."

Candice and I look at each other and giggle. "You may want to lower your expectations a little bit," I tell him.

Agent Taylor puts two twenty-dollar bills down on the table, then shoots me a concerned look. *Oh. Now he probably thinks his hotel is a dump.*

"It's a lovely hotel though!" I assure him. "Mrs. Winterling keeps the place in tip-top condition. You won't be upset with your accommodations."

"Thanks for paying, anyway," Candice says. *At least my sister has some manners.*

29

We part ways and head back home, and Candice and I sit down in the living room, waiting for Agent Taylor to arrive. I flick on the television. They're still showing footage of the wreckage recovery operation. Salvage cranes are lifting large chunks of the aircraft out of the ocean and into a ship's hold.

The crane comes up with another load, and this time it's the flight deck section. It's remarkably still intact. "Is that —?" Candice asks, and I nod.

"The cockpit windows," I confirm. "Dad would have been sitting right there when it happened." At the thought, I can feel tears burning my eyes.

I hear a car door slam. I stand up and watch through the window as Agent Taylor walks toward the house. I head for the front door and open it, waving him inside.

"Make yourself comfortable," I say as he follows me into the living room. He immediately starts snooping around, picking up various objects and feeling them.

"It's not bugged," I remark. I'm starting to get annoyed at him touching all our stuff.

"You never know, Miss Jette." Apparently satisfied, Agent Taylor takes a seat in the opposite chair. He reaches into his briefcase and pulls out a thick file that's practically bursting with paperwork.

"That's all for *us?*" I gape. "What are we, a couple of criminal masterminds?"

He opens his file and glances at me. "Just doing my job, Jackie," he says curtly.

"Sorry, I don't mean to be rude. I'm more nervous than anything. There's a random stranger from the government in my living room who's about to ask me if I know anything about my deceased father." I rub my hands together nervously, then place them on my knees. I shoot a glance at Candice, who looks just as nervous as I am.

"Certainly." He hands me a slim black file. "This is one of our numerous files on Agent Paul Jette, your father. I received clearance from my boss in Washington to inform you of this specific case so that you would believe what I'm about to tell you."

"And what are you about to tell us?" Candice interjects. "Dad was in the CIA? Dad was a secret agent?" She giggles, but I can tell she's anxious.

Agent Taylor raises one eyebrow. "Actually, your father had the gift of time travel."

He pauses to let us absorb what he's just said. "According to his handler, he hated time traveling, but he made good use of it to serve his country. I don't think we would have developed nearly so much military technology without him. And honestly, the transportation industry wouldn't be as safe as it is, either."

"Get out," I say.

"I beg your pardon?" Agent Taylor looks taken aback.

"Do you really think we're going to believe that? Do you have any proof?"

Candice places a hand on my knee. "Calm down, Jackie. I'm sure he has proof."

Agent Taylor shifts uncomfortably on his chair. "Please understand, I know how this sounds. Believe me, I thought it was crazy when I was chosen for this assignment, but now you see why I wanted to have this conversation in person and not over the phone."

"Hmmf." I'm not convinced, but I don't kick him out, either. "Please continue."

"Thank you." He straightens the papers on his lap. "I was sent here on special assignment, and the reason I wanted to speak with just you, Jackie, is because my boss wants to know if you possess your dad's same gift. Have you ever experienced time travel in the past?"

"Your boss wants to know *what*?" I repeat loudly. "That's absurd! That's downright crazy! How can anyone know how to time travel?"

Without a word, Agent Taylor reaches into his briefcase and removes another sheet of paper from other files, which he hands to me. Candice leans in so she can read it with me.

I study the document thoroughly. It seems Dad was asked to assist the Civil Aeronautics Board's Bureau of Aviation Safety, the predecessor to the NTSB, with the investigation of an earlier airline crash, one that went down in 1963.

Turns out, Dad learned a little more about himself when he touched a piece of the wreckage and ended up on an airplane to Cancún. "If the airplane crashed, how did Dad end up on the same aircraft? These documents are simply vague at best."

"Well, the documents are written for people who understand the assignment. Please allow me to clarify."

"Go ahead," I concede.

"Thank you. When Paul would touch a piece of the aircraft debris, he would be transported somehow through time, ultimately ending up on the aircraft before the crash occurred. For example, the crash in Cancún, he was on board the aircraft and he witnessed three men attempting to hijack it with handguns and other devices."

Candice jumped in. "If that was his first time acting as a time traveler, then how did he get back?"

Agent Taylor retrieves another document from his case. "According to this agent personnel file, your dad touched the same piece of wreckage as before. Luckily, the piece was located within the inner cabin area."

I jump in. "Where did he end up?"

The document goes on to describe that Paul was found in the field where the airplane went down. He was asleep and was awakened by a farmer who was working there.

"How did he know where to access the piece?" Candice asks. "If the flight was being overtaken by armed assailants, surely they would not permit him to mosey around the cabin."

Agent Taylor frowns. "Well, that's what we don't know in depth. Your father was very secretive, and he wouldn't tell anyone how he made it to the exact piece. But every time he reappeared; it was always at the crash site in present day."

I tilt my head to one side, skeptical. "And if the airplane crashed in the ocean? Where would he show up then?"

"That's a good question, Jackie." Agent Taylor shuffles through the papers in his briefcase, then pulls out another document. "Ah, here we go. On his second case, he was helping investigate a crash in the Atlantic Ocean."

Candice leans forward. "Well, what happened?"

His eyes scan the document, probably checking that he isn't saying anything classified. "Ah, here's what I wanted to find. *'Due to concerns from the classified agent, a special waterproof radio beacon will be added to the suit jacket. Once the suit contacts the water, the beacon has a range of four thousand miles and will alert ships in the area. Given that we know the coordinates of the crash site, a Navy vessel must be in a 25-mile radius. Once the beacon is received, such Navy vessel will dispatch a rescue chopper to pick up the package.'* That's how he survived."

"No." I spat. "That is how he would be *picked up* in the ocean."

Taken back by my remark, Agent Taylor frowns. "I'm afraid that I don't understand your question, or rather, your statement."

I uncross my legs to firm my position. "Agent Taylor, the Atlantic Ocean is freezing most of the year. How do you expect us to believe that our father could survive the frigid water while he waited for the rescue?"

I am growing particularly tired of his nonsense. The information he is providing sounds like the plot for a Stephen King novel. My temper tries to get the better of me, but I still let him try and explain. "Please continue, Agent."

Agent Taylor announced. "Whenever Paul touched a piece of airplane wreckage, he disappeared for twelve, sixteen, twenty hours or more. When he returned, he would somehow be in the exact location of where the plane had crashed."

I shake my head. "I'm sorry, Mr. Taylor, but I don't believe that."

"Ms. Jette, if you would allow me to finish speaking before you interrupt me, then maybe you would learn something," Agent Taylor barked.

Realizing that he was right put a taste like vinegar in my mouth. If he just had some proof of how Dad could survive in the cold water for more than the normal time it takes to freeze to death from hypothermia, then I would be satisfied.

Candice invites herself to ask the same question in a different manner. "Mr. Taylor, what I think that my sister is having difficulty with is, while Dad would wait in the near-freezing water for a rescue, how would he delay the hypothermia from taking effect? For example, was his suit similar to a wet suit, designed to keep heat closer?"

"Ladies, let me look for one thing. I know his personnel file had another page." Digging around the now-unorganized file cabinet within his briefcase, he retrieves another paper. Instead of reading it to us, he hands it over to me.

I read it over while Candice reads over my shoulder. "These are design sketches?" I muttered. As I read further down the paper, I understand the sketch is for Dad's suit, specifically a water suit.

I sat the paper down in front of me, now realizing that dad was given custom-made outfits for his mission. The specific suit would have a layer underneath, similar to a wetsuit, but this was more of a military grade.

Swallowing the vinegar, I relax my pose. "My apologies for doubting the information you presented." I feel terrible for being such a witch to him, but there are so many scammers in the world, and this whole ordeal is difficult to believe.

Moving on, I develop another question. "Why did the NTSB ask our dad to help with an investigation?"

Agent Taylor shares from another document — his briefcase resembles the never-ending storage capacity similar to the bag carried by a nanny with a talking umbrella. Turns out, Dad and a few of his classmates were invited to the Cancún wreck site for a learning assignment. The aircraft involved was a competitor's prototype of the Boeing 707.

The pilot training class was allowed to learn from the mistake alongside with the officials from Boeing. Once again, the documents are a little vague.

"What did his classmates do when he vanished after touching a piece of the broken airplane?" I ask.

"I am not sure, and there is no documentation about conversations held upon his departure or arrival at the crash site, but what I do know is Paul was sent to the Pentagon after for questioning, when an employee for the Secretary of Defense was advised of what happened by an anonymous source. After nearly a week of being held, Paul was sent back to New York to resume his career as a commercial pilot."

"Do you know what Americonic said when he returned?" I ask, as I'm sure that the airline was upset by his weeklong absence.

"No questions were asked." His simple response to my question informs me that Americonic was in cahoots with the government. Any employer would have terminated the employee for much less.

I rise from my seat and walk into the kitchen. Before walking too far, I turn around facing Candice and the agent. "Does anyone else need something to wash this down with?" I ask. Both nod their heads. I grab a bottle of wine for my sister and me along with two glasses. Agent Taylor can stick with bottled water.

I make my way back into the living room and set the tray down on the coffee table. Once we fill our glasses, I nod at Agent Taylor to continue.

"Now, where was I?" he says. "Oh yes, after an investigation, Paul was hired to work on top secret assignments, many of which are still used today. The knowledge he gave us helped us ensure people's safety and protected our national security. You can see now why the Pentagon has been so interested in you for all these years."

"Just how long has the government been watching — I mean, *interested in* my sister and me?" I demand. "And more importantly, why did they wait until I was fifty-two years old to spring this on me?"

"Well, Mr. Jenkins has been keeping a watch —"

Before he can say another word, I interrupt. "*Who* did you just say? You did *not* just say Mr. Jenkins! That's the name of the lawyer I work for."

"That's correct. When you lost your job in the late 1990s, Mr. Jenkins thought it would be a great way to keep an eye on you. Since you had no law experience, we could send you files, and you would never know the difference."

"How did he access confidential law files?" I ask, knowing how important client confidentiality is.

"After your father disappeared in 1971, Agent Jenkins was advised to keep a close eye on you for the duration of his career, but he was not allowed to make a move until you did. He was tasked with becoming a lawyer and building a legit law firm to prepare for your arrival in the late 1990s.

Candice chimes in. "That seems like a lot of work for such a simple result." By Mr. Jenkins becoming a legalized lawyer, Agent Taylor explained he was able to stay busy and draw a paycheck from the government and the law firm. What I still don't understand is why they waited all of these years to inform me. I asked Mr. Taylor for more clarification.

"He was under strict orders to document your existence and not engage with anything time travel related." Agent Taylor adjusts his body. "When top-level agents received word of the USS Lavon locating the aircraft debris, my team and Mr. Jenkins were informed and advised that we were to *initiate and engage the subject.* Meaning you, Jackie."

Now that I understand Mr. Jenkins a little more, I request Agent Taylor to tell us more about his role with our father. Turns out that Mr. Jenkins was assigned by high-ranking leaders within the Pentagon to be his handler in 1969 after Dad requested a permanent agent and not a bunch of different one's week after week. Not familiar with the term, Candice gladly asks what that means.

"Handler is similar to a business manager. They handle the paperwork, meetings, flights, et cetera. He also worked at the airport and assisted with Americonic crew scheduling in New York. Handled travel arrangements from one assignment to another and advised Americonic on scheduling reroutes in order to get Paul to the site of a crash or to a nearby government building where the wreckage was being secured. Often, he would be rerouted at the last minute, even if it caused a delay to the airline's operation."

Candice nudges me. "Jackie, your boss was Dad's handler back in the day! How cool is that?" Then to Agent Taylor, she asks, "Why are you only interested in my sister? We're both related to him."

At this, he looks grim. "Actually, you're not. You're adopted, Candice."

Candice raises her eyebrows and bats her eyes, confused. "What? No, I'm not adopted."

Agent Taylor pulls out a blue folder, from which he removes a golden yellowed paper which appears to be ancient as the paper appears brittle. I snatch it from his hands careful not to tear it.

"What kind of cruel joke is this?" I say before I start to read it.

Not amused, Agent Taylor says, "The piece of paper is the original 1953 birth certificate for a Candice Carter. Born to Charles and Christine Carter."

Together, we scan the document confirming his words. "He's right. Look, the birth parents are different. It's not Mom and Dad's names," Candice says.

I grow defensive with Agent Taylor again. "How do you expect us to believe that this brittle crumbling paper is real and not something that you or your team forged?" By this time, he had taken out another paper with similar yellowing though not as brittle. He handed it to us, and it had *ADOPTION CERTIFICATE* titled across the top. As we read the page, the listed parents were Paul and Beverly Jette, while the birth parents were marked as deceased.

"So, Candice was born to a couple in *London*? On July 23, *1953*? How do you explain that? What happened to those people?" Beside me, Candice says nothing. I think she's too shocked to speak.

Agent Taylor pulls out yet another document and reads. "Agent Jette returned to the present day, 1971, with a six-month-old baby girl. Upon his return, an investigation commenced, and it led to the determination that while Agent Jette was on assignment for information on a 1953 crash outside of London, he saved a passenger from the crash."

"If Dad saved me, why could he not save the other passengers from a tragic demise?" Candice asks as tears form in both of her eyes.

Agent Taylor face is grim and the next words from his mouth are admirable. "Paul was forbidden to save anyone. He was to observe and document only, as the government feared that a paradox would happen."

"Paradox?" I murmured as I am not familiar with that word.

"It can be a confusing word, so I will break it down," he says confidently. "A paradox is when a person time-travels and changes the course of history. For example, if you went back and tried to prevent

Patient Zero from getting the Spanish flu, you might succeed in saving that patient, but then you could catch it or someone else. History will always find a way even if you try and change it. That is the theory, and the government did not want to confirm that theory as it could jeopardize worldwide safety and security."

"I was born in 1953! What the *hell?* How do you just drop that on someone?" Candice shouts and storms off into the kitchen. I hear the refrigerator open as the glassware in the door slot clinks together. I lift from my seat and see her with another bottle of wine through the window above the counter. She pulls out the cork and doesn't even bother to pour it into a glass. Taking a three-second gulp from the bottle, she replaces it in the fridge and returns to the living room. "Okay, I'm back."

"I have a larger file with more information about your birth family back in Washington. We can plan to view it in the future if you wish."

Before he can continue, his phone starts to ring. He tells us to wait a second, and he answers the call. "Hello, this is Agent Taylor. Yes ma'am, I'm here now. Everything is going as projected. Is that right? Roger. I'll advise them. Goodbye." He hangs up the phone and turns his attention back to us.

"Who was that?" Candice asks, then she hesitates. "Wait, can I ask that?"

"This not the movies, Miss Jette." He smiles thinly. "That was my boss. She says they've just received the first shipment of the wreckage at the hangar in Washington."

"I thought the wreckage would be stored in Nova Scotia," I clarify.

"The larger pieces, yes. But these are small fragments that we can run tests on." He pauses for a moment and then says, "Actually, one of the tests we'd like to run is on *you*."

"Oh, I get it. You want me to touch a piece and see if I time travel, right?"

He nods. "Would you both be able to accompany me to Washington tomorrow?

"No way!" Candice hates long drives, and I feel the same way. It would take us all day to drive to Washington.

But Agent Taylor has other ideas. "No, no. I'll have a private plane chartered. The closest airfield is twenty miles away. Then, when I bring you both home, I'll drive back."

"You mean that old abandoned airfield, outside of town? That place belongs in an episode of *Murder, She Wrote*. How can you land a jet there?" I ask.

"The pavement's still in good condition. The Coast Guard uses the landing strip for practice at least three times a month."

Agent Taylor gathers his things, and we agree to meet the following morning at 10 a.m. sharp. I walk him to the door, while Candice retreats to the kitchen.

When I go back and join her, I find her hunched over the kitchen table, crying.

"Oh, Candice," I say, sitting down next to her and rubbing her back. "It's a lot, isn't it?"

"Dad took me twenty years into the future. He saved me from maybe dying in that crash with my biological parents. How can I *not* cry?"

"You're not mad at him?"

"Not one bit! I'm just happy that I got to live and be your sister." She wipes her tears, and we go back to the living room, and reminisce about the documents and information presented by Agent Taylor over the day.

CHAPTER 3

1971, Paul's last day...

On a beautiful August morning, the birds whistle from the massive red maple trees in the front yard. The rose bushes hum with bumblebees working their way around the red and yellow petals.

The Craftsman-style bungalow is nestled in a generous, neatly trimmed lawn, dozens of different colored rose bushes lining the red brick walkway from the white picket fence up to the house. The house is built of red brick, with wood siding near the roofline.

Large wind chimes hang from the porch, each playing a different musical number as they sway in the wind. White rocking chairs give the porch a welcoming feel, inviting guest to sit back and enjoy themselves.

From inside the house, Paul and his wife, Beverly, are in their bedroom, conversing about Paul's upcoming trip to Rome. Beverly sits in the large wingback chair in front of the window overlooking the yard. Paul is standing in front of the heavy wood dresser, looking for his gold watch. Worried, he turns to his wife. "Honey, have you seen it?"

Snapping back from her daydream, she replies, "Yes, I had a new battery put in yesterday. Let me grab it from my purse." Beverly leaves the bedroom and goes to the foyer, reaching in her purse. She pulls out the Pearl-Norms jewelry shop case and smiles. She's filled with the memory of giving Paul this watch on the day he earned his captain stripes, nearly five years ago.

Upon her return to the bedroom, she sees Paul pinning his golden captain's wings onto his white uniform shirt. She stands in the doorway, leaning against the door frame. He turns and admires her, standing in a pale blue housecoat with her curly blonde hair pinned up.

"What?" Paul asks, as he wiggles his arms through his blazer.

"You look so handsome. Those flight attendants won't be able to keep their hands off you," Beverly remarks casually as she walks toward Paul. "Here's your watch."

"Now, honey, you know I only have eyes for you." Paul extends his left arm, and she secures the watch around his wrist and fastens the band.

"I know, I just wanted to hear you say it," Beverly laughs, walking to the side of the bed to close the lid on his red and gold airline suitcase. "Paul, this feels light."

"Well, I need room for Jackie and Candice's snow globes, and maybe a surprise for you, dear. Thank you for having the battery replaced. Flying over the Atlantic without a watch would not be good."

The couple laughs together. Paul grabs his suitcase and makes his way to the front door. She follows him, exiting the bedroom, heading down the white-carpeted hallway lined with family photos of present and past generations of the Jette Family.

Before reaching the foyer at the end of the hallway, Paul peeks his head into the girls' room. The home is big enough for the girls to have their own separate rooms, but because they are little, Beverly thought it best for them to be in the same room. Jackie is playing with some building blocks on the floor. Candice is cuddling her favorite stuffed animal which she named Maddie — the doggy protector. Paul purchased Maddie on a trip to Denver a few weeks ago.

Paul heads into their room and sets his suitcase on the floor. Jackie's face lights up with a big smile, just like every time she sees her dad. He reaches down to pick her up, giving the biggest smooch and asking, "Now is Daddy's big girl going to be Mommy's little helper while I'm gone?"

Still holding a building block in her hand, she smiles, nodding her head. He turns around and points to the wall, which is filled with snow globes from many of the fabulous faraway places that he has visited. He asks if she would like one from Rome. She nods again, hoping for a new present. He promises, then places her on the pink and brown quilt on the bed. She slides down the quilt and returns to building the castle from earlier.

Paul then steps over to Candice's crib. She's fallen asleep holding Maddie. He leans into the crib and gives her a kiss on the cheek, careful not to wake her. He straightens, then reaches down to pick up his suitcase.

Beverly has been watching from the doorway the entire time. When he leaves the girls' room, she closes the door and follows Paul out to the foyer. He takes one last look at himself in the mirror and repositions his gold-embroidered cap. Mom opens the front door for him, careful not to rumple his uniform.

As they both walk onto the porch, she asks him if he has everything he needs for the trip. Our mother used to worry about airplanes flying nearly four miles high, six hundred miles an hour, but now she's used to it — it's her every day, normal routine.

Giving her a kiss goodbye, Paul heads down the front steps to his car, a 1970 Buick Electra which he's nicknamed "Amelia" after Amelia Earhart's Lockheed Electra.

Unlocking the driver's side door, he places his briefcase — full of the usual pilot necessities such as a flashlight with extra batteries, sunglasses and other informational books about aviation — and his small suitcase on the blue leather passenger seat and climbs inside.

He pumps the gas and inserts the key in the ignition. The car roars to life and he shifts into reverse and backs down the driveway. Once in the street, he honks twice to say goodbye and off he goes, driving towards the airport.

As he speeds down the expressway toward John F. Kennedy International Airport, the radio is playing, but he's not listening to the music. Instead, he's daydreaming about coming back home to his family after this three-day trip to Rome. The girls — meaning his wife and two daughters — love the little surprise gifts he brings them from all the fabulous faraway places he visits. On his last trip, he brought home some diamond earrings from the Let-Gal jewelry store in London, and Beverly couldn't wait to show them off at her bridge club the following week.

Approaching the airport, his eyes rest on the Americonic Aircove terminal. The traffic is moderate, as he's arrived before the rush. As he pulls up to the garage at the end of the terminal, he admires the bright neon Americonic signage on the side of the building. On both sides of the terminal, you can see the tails rising above the perimeter fencing. After all, the tails stand six to seven stories above the ground.

The lavish Aircove terminal is designed like a flying saucer, very majestic for its time. The front grass area contains a dozen impressive sculptures that represent the history of flight, from the Wright brothers to the first jetliner. Mixed in with the sculptures are flag poles flying the flags of every nation Americonic travels to. An impressive sight and great advertisement.

Upon entering the Aircove terminal, the ceiling is held up high by opulent columns surrounding the perimeter of the terminal. Paul walks over the dark navy blue carpet that spans the entire terminal. Stamped within the carpet are mini aircraft flying around the floor in a light shade of blue. He passes the four marble plated counters where passengers can check their luggage to their final destination. He stops by the large departure board — a large sculpture broadcasting arrivals too — double checking his flight to Rome. *On time! Just what I like to see.*

Beyond the departure board, there are a variety of restaurants for customers to indulge and watch the aircraft landing and departing. Looking around, the French restaurant seems busier than the coffee shop. The windows inside of the eatery are enormous, and you can see airplanes landing and taking off throughout the day. Paul continues on his quest to the Pilot and flight attendant offices.

An enormous gift shop fills the middle of the terminal, stocked with every essential that a passenger or crew member would need. The windows outside of the shop stand brilliant with Americonic International tote bags, pins, toy airplanes and more airline branded items.

Paul peeks in the shop and looks over to the candy island. He purchases a goody bag for his crew, filled with chocolates, mints and more.

Paul arrives at the crew lounge in the rear of the terminal. From this office, crews can plan their flights, communicate with operations and with the Americonic Building in New York. He enters through the spinning door and proceeds down the hall to the check-in desk. The walls are painted white and hold a treasure of pictures including the airline's first aircraft, a Lockheed Constellation with the triple tail.

Susie Jenkins, the receptionist, sees Paul approaching her from behind a large desk. She looks down at her notes and sees that Paul is the captain on Flight 329 to Rome. She puts a check mark next to his name and inks the time he checked in.

"Hello, Captain Paul, you're right on time like always," she greets him. "Your first officer and flight engineer arrived a few minutes ago, and they're waiting in Briefing Room 3."

"How are you today, gorgeous?" Paul flirts, and Susie responds by giggling.

"How's that beautiful wife and kids of yours, Paul?" She lays out the flight documents on the countertop.

"Beverly's great. She's at home with the kids. I already have my shopping list for Rome. How is your husband doing?"

"Fine, but he's always working. He said for me to tell you that he'll meet you on the concourse before boarding." Susie shifts the paperwork on the counter to make sure it's stacked evenly.

Looking at the neatly stack paperwork, Paul suggests that Suzie apply for the flight attendant position that recently opened up, given that she has expertise with airline crews, route schedules and knows most of the flight attendants who are based here.

Paul grabs all his stuff from the counter, smiles and proceeds down the hall. Walking past the offices, he arrives at Door 3 and knocks, even though it's already open. "Hello, gentlemen, how's everything going?" he asks.

The two other pilots rise from their seats in greeting. Dan, the first officer, shakes Paul's hand and advises him that the dispatcher will be in momentarily to brief them.

Paul then turns his head to the flight engineer, Ray. Extending his hand, Paul tells Ray he's heard a great deal about him. "Great to have you on the crew," he says.

The men all converse for a few minutes, before their attention is captured by the dispatch agent who enters the room with a portfolio. His greets the men and introduces himself as Randy.

Randy sits down at the mahogany briefing table, pulling out all his paperwork. "I don't see any weather at this time," he reports. "Should be clear skies and smooth the whole way there." He hands the release to Paul. "Captain, if you look at the remarks section, I've added a note about the aft cargo door."

Before he reads the remark, Paul turns to Randy. "I've got a good bird today, right?"

"Yes, sir." Randy says and points to the remarks. "Maintenance worked all morning to replace the hinges and locking mechanisms, just to be safe."

"Sounds safe to me." Paul says and continues to read. One thing that catches Paul by surprise is the cargo manifest. The cargo is listed as MILITARY GRADE. "What's this about?" he asks. "We're not flying rocket launchers, are we?"

"Uncle Sam's shipping a bunch of dry and canned goods to military camps in Vietnam. That MILITARY GRADE just refers to the food," Randy clarifies. "No HAZMAT will be flying this leg. We'll send that on the cargo charter on Friday."

Once Randy completes the briefing, Paul signs the paperwork per regulation protocols. Randy wishes them a great trip and leaves the room to file the documents.

As the men leave the briefing room, they stand outside of a second office. Peeking their heads inside, the flight attendants on tonight's flight are meeting with their inflight supervisor, Lona Lilliana, to talk about any special dietary needs on board and for a small safety refresher.

The attendants are dressed to impress in their dark navy dresses with matching jackets and pillbox hats. Underneath the tiny hats, their hair is neat and well kept. They each have a matching American flag scarf tied around their petite necks in a perfect bow.

When Lona concludes the safety topics, Marge, the lead purser with an elegant British accent, responds first. "Mrs. Lilliana, is it true that we have a new jet?"

"Yes! This aircraft is just a few months old. There shouldn't be a nick or a scratch in the galley, and I expect you'll keep it that way. As corporate scraps those old and worn-out birds, we need to take care of these new ones as they will be in our fleet for the next 20 years. You're familiar with the safety features on the 707?"

Lona pauses for a moment and notices a rip in Cheryl's stocking. "Miss Gowan, I trust you have a new pair of stockings in your bag to change into?"

The new flight attendant turns beet red and mumbles, "Yes, ma'am. I'll change right after our briefing."

Lona smiles and nods. "Very good." Directing her attention back to the group, she asks again, "Are you all up to date on the 707 safety features?"

The ladies respond and nod their heads in acknowledgment. Lona passes around the flight information for her crew to review the details about the flight and their destination, should a passenger ask them.

"Marge, here's your crew and passenger manifest." Marge takes the document and looks it over while Lona continues about safety and other related topics, quizzing each lady on a variety of regulations and protocols. Once the briefing is finished, she asks all the women to stand for grooming checks. Lona is known for her exacting appearance standards. Some of the flight attendants call her Lona Lovely.

After the supervisor corrects a few infractions, the well-styled ladies sign the crew sheet for Lona's records, and they're ready to head up to the gate.

As senior purser, Marge assigns each woman's position. Judy will assist Marge in the first-class section. Gail is the second purser on the fight and oversees the tourist class. Cheryl, Charlene, and Mary will serve with her.

Before Lona leaves the briefing room, she tells everyone to have a great flight. The crew grab their luggage and blue Americonic handbags. As they walk down the hallway, they encounter Captain Jette and the other two pilots, standing near the exit, talking shop. The men go quiet when they notice the women walking towards them.

Captain Jette greets them. "Hello, ladies. All finished with your briefing?"

Marge speaks for the crew. "Hello, Captain, yes! All done, and we're heading up to Gate 6. Care to join us?"

"Sure, and since we're all together here, why don't I brief you here." The ladies nod and Captain Paul begins.

"We have a good flight ahead of us. The is a newer aircraft, and we have a great crew here today. We'll have 93 passengers on board. I expect a smooth ride once we get to our cruising altitude of 37,000 feet. I'll call back once I believe it's all clear, so you can start serving dinner.

Should anything change, I'll let you know. Remember, everyone, we're the face of the airline, and people want to have a good experience. *Smile.* If any issues arrive, let me know and I will address the problem."

Paul finishes his briefing, and they exit the crew lounge through the glass doors. As they walk together from the lounge, passengers stare at the group in their custom-made uniforms. The crowd parts like the Red Sea. The concessions are stuffed to the brim with passengers trying to get one last snack in before their flights, and the waitresses rush around in their beautiful blue smocks and matching pillbox hats.

Paul shakes his head. *Why are people buying food when we serve a full meal and snacks on the flight?* He smiles and laughs to himself as they approach the gate.

The flight crew arrives at the gate and peers through the large windows at the aircraft sitting on the gate pad. Gail lets out a low whistle. "Wow! That is the most beautiful plane I've ever seen!"

"She sure is!" Paul agrees. "That new paint job is breathtaking."

Beginning on the belly of the aircraft, aft of the wings, are dozens of red, white, blue and silver stars. As the stars make their way up to the tip of the tail fin, they give the impression that the aircraft is flying through a brilliant night sky.

A man arrives at the gate and approaches Paul. He's wearing a black suit coat with a blue striped tie that complements the Americonic logo. He also has a name badge.

"Hello, Captain Jette. I'm sure you're aware we have a celebrity onboard, and I'm here to ensure the boarding process is smooth for our special guest."

"Hello, Jenkins, good to see you again! How are operations going?"

"Likewise! Same operation, different flight." Mr. Jenkins chuckles as he continues. "Our CEO wants to make sure we get only good press on this flight. I hope I won't be a bother to anyone."

"Of course." Paul turns to Marge. "Marge, I'm sure our guest will be most comfortable with you and the girls today."

Marge reviews her paperwork. "Mr. Jenkins, I'm looking over the first-class manifest and I don't see any famous names listed?"

"That's correct, Miss Carter," Mr. Jenkins nods. "Our special guest is traveling under her real name, not her stage name. The name on the manifest is Carol LaBryant. I believe the name she uses on stage is Lorraine Reynolds."

The flight crew's mouths all drop open with shock. Marge is the first one to speak.

"LORRAINE REYNOLDS? *The* Lorraine Reynolds from the hit TV show, *Lorraine's Hour?* No *way!*"

"And that's why stars use their birth names on the manifest," Mr. Jenkins confirms. "She'll be in seat 6A with her manager, Mrs. PennWell, in seat 6B. Please make sure we give them our best first-class experience."

The team all nod their heads in agreement. At the same moment, the operations agent arrives to open the terminal door and give Paul the updated weather information. "Captain, the weather looks good all the way to Rome. Shouldn't be an issue."

"Thank you, Teri." Paul takes the paperwork from her with a polite smile. Mr. Jenkins walks away towards the first-class lounge. Teri gives the pilots a small briefing about the boarding and advises that everything looks on time.

"Sounds good, Teri." Paul replies and starts walking down the Jetway to the aircraft, the rest of the crew close behind him. The Jetway is lined with travel posters advertising the airlines new destinations and new jets that are arriving weekly from the manufacturer in Seattle.

He arrives at the bottom and sees the aircraft door is open. Paul is the first to enter the airplane. The forward entry door — L1 — is already open, since catering and cleaning crews have just left. He can already smell the scent of a new airplane.

Stepping into the cabin, he turns to the left and enters the empty flight deck. Placing his briefcase and other items in the jump seat located behind the captain's chair, he flips a few switches, and the plane's interior flickers eventually lights up bright.

Ray stows his luggage, then grabs a pair of earplugs from his coat pocket. He steps out into the jetway and down to the ramp via a side door to complete his safety walk-around, as he does before every flight.

The rest of the flight crew steps onto the plane behind Paul. Marge and the other flight attendants take a moment to admire the aircraft. The forward cabin has a half-round lounge for customers to use in flight.

The interior is absolutely stunning, with immaculate blue and white upholstery. The overhead storage areas have small televisions spaced out through the cabin, an Americonic innovation. The passengers appreciate the distraction from the long flight time.

Shortly after stowing her items, Marge starts opening cabinets and checking her safety equipment. Judy inspects the first-class galley and begins pouring small flutes of champagne in gold crested glassware with an eagle on the side and the AIA logo on the other.

Ray steps into the flight deck. He takes a seat at his desk surrounded by the gauges displaying fuel quantities, hydraulic fluid level, and even the cabin temperature controls. He declares, "This beauty looks good! I didn't see any issues. Not even a blemish."

Paul stands up and nods. "Okay, I'm taking a walk. If I find anything you missed, you're buying the steaks in Rome."

The three pilots laugh, and Paul exits the airplane but runs into Mr. Jenkins before he can head down the stairs.

The two men speak discreetly and Mr. Jenkins hands him an envelope, which Paul slips into his inside blazer pocket. Mr. Jenkins returns to the passenger boarding area and Paul begins his walk around, inspecting the aircraft with a stern eye. His attention is diverted when he sees the ground agents loading a bunch of cargo. He stops at the aft cargo bin to speak with them.

"Say, gentlemen, what are in all of those boxes?"

The lead ramp agent — identified by the word LEAD in large white letters on his shirt back, turns around, startled by the question.

"Howdy, Captain!" he says. "These wooden crates are for the US Army. Everything is headed for Vietnam on the 215 flight from Rome tomorrow. They arrived from the base at the last minute. The cargo manifest listed it as surplus supplies from World War Two."

"What supplies? Mind if I see the cargo manifest for myself?" The ramp loading agent hands the clipboard to Paul. "When I see DO NOT OPEN and US MILITARY on the same boxes, that concerns me."

Paul reviews the paperwork as he wants to see what is inside of the cargo containers. According to the listed items, they are surplus military helmets, jackets and more wearable items for military personnel in the field.

Relieved, Paul returns the clipboard and the ramp continues to load the aircraft. When he re-renters the aircraft, Marge greets the captain with a flirtatious mini-salute. "Captain, we're ready to board!"

"Thank you, Marge." He cocks his head. "Sounds like customers are arriving now."

Marge picks up the interphone and announces, "Boarding." The other flight attendants take their positions.

Paul returns to the flight deck. "Well, Ray, you lucky bastard, the walk around was good." The men all laugh and carry on with their checklists.

Mr. Jenkins arrives at the forward boarding door with Lorraine Reynolds and her assistant. Marge greets both of them with a poised smile. "Marge," Mr. Jenkins says, "this is Carol LaBryant. She'll be traveling with her manager today."

"Welcome aboard, Miss LaBryant," Marge greets her. "I hope you enjoy your flight with us today. Should you need anything, please don't hesitate to ask."

Mr. Jenkins walks them both down the aisle and shows them to their seats, as Marge shakes her head, incredulous. *That's a major television star, wow!*

As the boarding process continues, Mr. Jenkins exits the aircraft and returns to his duties in the terminal. The passenger's stream in slowly as they try to soak in that new airplane smell. Many are excited to travel and dressed in their Sunday best for the flight. The flight attendants help customers navigate the cabin and show them to their assigned seats. As customers remove their jackets and blazers, each attendant writes the seat number on a mini tag before hanging them in the coat closets.

Judy passes out the complimentary pre-departure champagne to the first-class customers while Gail and Cheryl assist families with their children. Two unaccompanied children arrive with the gate agent Teri. Marge escorts them to row 10 so that she can keep an eye on them during the flight.

"Cindy, George, my name is Marge, and I have a secret to tell you." Both children are riddled with suspense as they lean in closer to Marge who has squatted down to be on the same level. Marge whispers, "My galley is filled with a ton of snacks and drinks just for you two. If you need anything, please ring this little button here." She points and presses the button which illuminates a small light bulb next to it and sounds a bell to alert her.

Cindy and George nod their heads in excitement and Marge returns to her boarding duties. Before she can reach the front boarding door, the bell sounds, and she looks back to see the children giggling.

As boarding comes to a close, the flight attendants go through the cabin making sure all of the galleys are buttoned up tight for takeoff. Once Teri closes the forward boarding door, Marge begins the in-flight safety announcements while the three remaining attendants stand in the aisle demonstrating the safety features of the Boeing 707.

The pilots are cleared to start the engines, and the airplane pushes back from the gate. As the sun begins to set in New York, Marge peeks her head into the cockpit. "Captain, we are all secured back here. I'll pop in once we get up."

"Thank you, Marge. Do the passengers seem excited to fly on this new jet?"

Marge smiles at the question. "Yes, they are all glued to their windows for the take-off." Many of them have never had the privilege of flying before.

While they wait for takeoff clearance, Paul decides to take a moment and make an announcement when Marge exits.

"Ladies and Gentlemen," he says, "We are waiting for takeoff clearance from the tower, and we should be underway here shortly. Make sure to keep your eyes fixated on the city lights as we lift off the ground and climb into the air. Thank you for flying with us today."

The tower contacts the aircraft soon after and permits the takeoff. Golden glows light up the rear tailpipes of the creature's four engines as the throttles are moved forward in the cockpit. The vibration from the four engines roars through the cabin. Moments later, the brakes are released, and the Boeing 707 begins its roll down the runway.

As the large jetliner accelerates down the runway, Paul has control of the steering and his right hand on the throttle, pushing them to max takeoff thrust. The idea that he holds the power to this aircraft all in the movement of his fingers arouses his ego.

The throttles have reached their max position on the quadrant, and his arm returns to the yoke while the first officer keeps watch of the speed and calls out the desired checkpoints. He calls out. "V1."

Paul acknowledges, and the aircraft keeps rolling down the runway, nearing liftoff speed.

The first office then calls out, "Rotate." The captain acknowledges and pulls back slightly on the control column. The magnificent creature racing down the runway responds gently, and the nose gear lifts off the ground, followed by the main gear. After a few more seconds, the ground grows smaller and the 707 climbs into the evening sky.

CHAPTER 4

Present day 2023, in the home of Candice and Jackie Jette.

The night has passed so quickly since Agent Taylor left earlier. Candice and I finished off the cheap wine and decided that it was time to put this conversation in a holding pattern for the night.

I get up to get ready for bed, stopping in the kitchen to place my empty wine glass in the sink. We lock up the house and head upstairs to our bedrooms.

What an exhausting day. I fall quickly into a dreamless sleep.

The next morning, we are awakened by a pounding at the front door. Startled from my sleep, I jump out of bed and pull back the curtains. Agent Taylor's black SUV is in the driveway.

I walk back to my phone, double-tap the screen, and see it's nearly 9 a.m. I run across the hall and bang on Candice's door to wake her. "SIS! Get up, he's already here!"

I race back to my room and head for the closet. I throw on a blouse, sweater and pants, and pull my hair back in a ponytail. Hurrying out my door and down the stairs, I unlock the front door.

"Almost ready!" I call out breathlessly. "Take a seat in a rocking chair; we'll be right there!"

Canadice is already making coffee. "Make me one, will you?" I run around grabbing purses, tablets and chargers. Caffeinated and ready, we finally step out of the front door.

"Ladies," Agent Taylor greets us. "Your airplane awaits."

I hop into the front seat of his SUV, and Candice sits in back. Oddly enough, I feel sad to see the house get smaller and smaller as we drive away. *I'm such a homebody.* My stomach is in knots as we cruise down the road to the airfield.

"So, what's the plan for today?" I ask, since no one else is talking.

"Once we land in Washington, we'll have an early lunch. The flight should only be about an hour. There's a good café at the office. After lunch, my boss wants to meet with all of us before we dive into your dad's files. How does that sound?"

"Busy," I say, inwardly groaning at the thought of the long day ahead of us.

"The jet will take you back home as soon as we're done," Agent Taylor reassures me.

There are no gates or security at the old airfield, but a small plane is parked at one end of the runway. Agent Taylor drives right up to the aircraft. Throwing the car into park, he says "We're here."

In the back seat, Candice wakes up from her nap. We step out of the car and head up the stairs to the aircraft, where the pilot greets us. Most pilots wear the black pants with the white shirt and gold stripes displaying their rank. Our pilot today is wearing green baggy flight suit.

I learn over and whisper. "Agent Taylor, is this a private jet or one from the Air Force?"

He giggles. "Very good observation. This is a charter Air Force jet. We have a discretionary fund to use it a few times a year. And today is a special occasion fifty-one years in the making."

I ask the pilot what the in-flight movie will be, and he laughs. "Today, we're featuring *Up in the Air.*" He gestures to us to take our seats. This is like no jetliner I've ever been on in the past. It only has four seats in the cabin, and two pilots up front.

The three of us get settled, and in a few minutes, we're taxiing down the runway. Fifty-six minutes later, we land at Andrews Air Force Base. The engines purr as we cruise to our gate and stop.

On the tarmac, we're greeted by another black SUV and Air Force officials in full uniform. Agent Taylor greets them both with a handshake. I take it they know each other.

"Ladies, welcome to Washington," he says as he opens the back door of the car for us. We get in, and soon we arrive at a hangar on the other end of the air base.

"What are we doing here?" Candice asks.

"My boss requested that we meet here to discuss your dad in a secure area."

"What about lunch?" Candice wants to know.

"We'll have something sent over from the café," Agent Taylor replies.

Upon entering the building, we walk down a series of hallways and arrive at a lavish office, with white walls and a richly stained coffee table that is accompanied by a set of four seafoam green swivel chairs with wooden bases that match the coffee table. Behind the chairs is an enormous white bookshelf that stretches from floor to ceiling with an electric fireplace in the middle.

"If you will please have a seat, she should be here in a few moments." Agent Taylor is on his phone, texting.

"She?" I ask, surprised that his boss is a woman.

Agent Taylor nods. "She has the best leadership skills of any commanding officer I've ever worked for."

After a few moments, a tall, attractive woman in her forties enters, pushing a rolling file box. "Hello, ladies, my name is Melinda Rodriguez, Lieutenant Colonel of the United States Air Force Aviation Research and Discovery department. I oversee special assignments for Andrews Air Force Base."

Both Candice and I look her up and down. She's wearing a grey pantsuit and an off-white blouse. Her hair is a dark, rich brown, and her face has never seen a day of Botox. Good genetics are in her favor. She also has the whitest teeth I've ever seen.

"It's a pleasure to meet you," I say. "That is a large title. Do you prefer Lieutenant Colonel Rodriguez or Melinda?"

"Melinda's perfectly fine. We're very informal these days." She takes a seat across from us at the gleaming black table.

"What about you, Agent Taylor?" Candice asks. "Do we have to keep calling you Agent Taylor or do you have a first name? I mean, we're talking about time travel here. Can't we drop the formalities?"

I snort, but Agent Taylor doesn't even crack a smile.

"Agent Taylor. Agent Taylor is my first name."

Melinda's sifting through her box of files, selecting several folders that have RESTRICTED ACCESS stamped on them in red.

"These are a handful of your dad's assignments," she starts. "I wanted to share them so that you have an understanding of just how important he was to our operation." She opens the first folder and begins to read. "This case ID TA01161942, completed on April 27, 1969. The agent is Paul Jette. The mission was to time travel and investigate the crash of Transwest Air Flight 300 on January 16, 1942. A piece of the aircraft was flown to Washington. He touched a small piece of the tail fin and was sent on board the aircraft as it climbed out of Las Vegas. During the first ten minutes that he was on board the plane, he experienced a routine flight. At the eleventh minute, a man stood in the cabin shouting the Nazi slogan, *'Ein volk, ein reich, ein Führer!'* which translates to 'One people, one realm, one leader.' The man stormed the flight deck, and the plane begin to change course. People were screaming in the cabin. At two minutes before impact, Agent Jette returned to the present day. As suspected, he returned to the crash site. Agent Jette shot a signal flare, and an Air Force helicopter retrieved him. Once in Washington, he relayed his findings to the NTSB, who then corrected the secret file but kept the original report the same."

Melinda closes the file and says, "Do you ladies have any questions about this case before we move on to the next one?"

"Yes," I say. "How did he get on the flight? Wouldn't a crew member or another passenger notice a man who wasn't there at takeoff? Also, what do the letters mean at the beginning of the case id?"

Melinda smiles. "Right on the nose, Jackie. You are correct. He showed up after takeoff. In fact, for every accident he investigated, he arrived in the cabin after takeoff. The letters represent the airline code. TA from Transwest Air, and this next one is AIA for Americonic International Airways."

Candice chimes in. "So, weren't people alarmed to see some guy just appear on the plane?"

Melinda picks up the second file. "I am positive that the site of a person appearing from nowhere is shocking, but the people on the airplane were going to die anyway. Once the plane was in the air, there was no proof that Agent Jette was ever on board. I don't mean that in a bad way. Paul is there to document history, not change it."

Before we can dig into the next file, Melinda's assistant arrives with our lunch, and she passes around the bags of sandwiches. Then she opens the second file.

This one looks a bit thicker than the last one. She opens it and begins to read. "This is case ID AIA05041957, complete on June 23, 1970. The agent is Paul Jette. The mission was to time travel and investigate what happened on Americonic Flight 237, a Boeing 377 Stratoliner in route to Honolulu from San Francisco on May 4, 1957. The aircraft went missing and was located on May 11, but no cause for the crash was found. Agent Jette touched a piece of the wreckage at Camp Pendleton in San Diego. He time traveled and appeared on the aircraft at 6pm local time. He observed an engine fire on the port side. The crew was passing out life vest and instructing passengers to remove their shoes to prepare for a water landing. Just before the plane hit the water, Agent Jette time traveled back to the present day. A navy vessel picked him up shortly after he returned." Melinda closes the file.

I put up one hand. "If an airplane crashes into the ocean, how did Dad survive?"

"According to his file, the team planned for a rescue at the exact coordinates of the crash. Paul was also equipped with a waterproof flare inside his coat pocket. As an extra safety measure, his jacket had a location beacon inside of it. Once saltwater touches the beacon, it sends a signal to the nearest aircraft or ship. I believe that Agent Taylor told you about his wetsuit material to keep him from freezing, but did he tell you that the blazer had built in flotation device?"

"No, but that explains how he could survive the large waves in the open sea," I noted.

"Yes, the amazing technology that we had back in the late sixties and seventies was so top secret. We could drop military assets in open water, and they would survive long enough for pick up. If our enemies found out, it would not have been good."

"So, how did our dad get access to the top-secret suit and flotations?" I inquired.

Melinda answered. "I am not sure, since Kenneth Gable was in charge before I took over in the nineties when he retired. I am confident when I say that our world is small and every connection you make is very important."

Noticing the silence, Melinda turns to my sister. "Candice? You're quiet. Is there anything you want to ask?"

"Well, yeah." She looks thoughtful. "We know that he would touch a piece of the wreckage, right? And he'd end up on the plane before it crashed. But then how would he get back to present day?"

"Fair point," I say. Truth is, I hadn't thought of that. And I'm the potential time traveler here.

"It's a lot simpler than it sounds. He would locate the same part and touch it again." Melinda responds.

"What if the piece isn't reachable during the flight?" I persist.

"For each mission, Agent Jette used an easily accessible interior part that any passenger could access, such as the lavatory mirror, seat cushions or frames, interior paneling, et cetera."

Candice frowns. "Why didn't he save the flight and the people if he knew what was going to happen?"

"It's not that easy. If a stranger were to show up midflight, shouting that the plane was about to crash, people would think he was crazy. Per orders from the Pentagon, he was to observe and not rescue as to not create a paradox. In Agent Taylor's summary from his visit, he listed that he explained what a paradox is, correct?"

"Mhmm." *Ugh. Leaving all those poor people to die. It must have been awful.* "What will my mission be?" I ask. "I mean, if I can time-travel. Which is a big if."

Melinda finishes her sandwich and wipes her hands on a paper napkin. "Well, Jackie, I don't want to scare you with the details, but I think you're capable of hearing them."

"I've been told that my father can time-travel, and that my sister was born in 1953 I can hear anything at this point," I tell her.

Melinda retrieves a third folder, this one green. "Why is the folder green?" I ask.

"Mission is a go," she tells me. "When a mission has approval to proceed, the folder changes from blue to green. Once the mission is completed, the folder is changed to red."

She pauses for a moment, looking from my sister to me. "Jackie, this mission is the most important. I must remind you that this, all of this, is confidential and no one outside of this room can know about our actions. Should these files be divulged outside of this room or a meeting with

Agent Taylor or myself, national security would be at risk. Do you agree?"

We nod, and she takes a paper out of the folder. She shows it to us, and I see the mission is coded AIA07062023.

AIA, the airline's initials and today's date. Is this one for me? I scan the document. It's a mission for me to time-travel and find out what happened to my dad's airplane.

My heart drops in my chest. "My first mission is to find out what happened to my dad's airplane?"

Melinda nods her head. "Well, the first mission is a mix. We need to see if you can time-travel — if you can't, then we will release these files, and you can return to your normal life in Bluefin Cove. The second half, if you can time-travel, is to find answers for something that my previous leader searched for years after the disappearance and found nothing."

"But the NTSB report said the search was called off," Candice points out.

"The White House told the press that. Given the fact that your father was on the aircraft, the Pentagon wanted the press away from the search."

I read through the document. Dad's plane went down in the Atlantic Ocean. *That means I'm going to end up in the water. In the exact place where he died.*

"You'll need to dress in period attire, of course. We have a personal appearance specialist that has designed an outfit for you to wear on your trip," Melinda says.

"Will it have the water beacon in it and a flotation?" Candice asks.

"Of course," Melinda tells her. "With today's technology, the Navy will have your sister's location within seconds and dispatch helicopters."

"How do I just appear on the plane? People are going to freak out." I say.

"We have a plan for that. Among the recovered wreckage, we have a lavatory mirror taken from a large chunk of the salvaged wreck. I want you to touch that. That way, you'll arrive in the lavatory and be able to blend in."

Agent Taylor, who's been silent until this point, finally speaks up. "People aren't as observant as you'd think. You'll be just fine. Besides, it should be dark outside. People will be sleeping or doing their own thing."

"And when do you want to do this, exactly? I mean, the wreckage is up in Nova Scotia, right?

Melinda glances at her phone. "It's 2 p.m. now. The mirror should be arriving in a few hours from Nova Scotia."

A surge of adrenaline jolts through me. *Today. They want me to do this today?*

"Yes," Melinda says, as though she read my mind. "I want to have you ready for testing by this time tomorrow."

"I have to think about this," I state to Melinda. What if I do get to 1971 and can't get back? There are so many questions I have and so many *what ifs. "*Can we have a moment?"

Melinda and Agent Taylor leave the room. Once they are gone, I speak with Candice about all of this. "What do you think?"

"Oh, no, Jackie," Candice says. "This is your life and I want you to make the decision. There are lots of risks, but imagine the opportunity to see Dad again."

"And what if I get stuck on that airplane?" I challenged.

"The chance that this will even work is like ten zillion to one," Candice chuckles.

I am not amused by her giggle. "And my luck, it will work."

"So, if it does, you know to touch the same piece and you will be back in present day. Jackie, you are my sister, and I love you, but this is a chance to explore a whole new world. Bluefin Cove will always be there."

Deciding that Candice made a compelling argument, I rise from my chair and open the door to find Melinda and Agent Taylor standing down the hallway. I wave at them to return and tell them that I will accept the assignment.

"Okay," Melinda states, "I'll send you off with Stephanie. She's going to get you dressed for the trip. As for you, Candice," she turns to my sister, "this folder contains everything about your birth parents who died in 1953. While your sister helps us, I want to help you explore your past."

There's a knock at the door. Agent Taylor, who is still standing, turns around to open it, and a woman walks in. She is stunning in her light blue petite safari-belted pantsuit. Her dirty blonde hair is in a bun that is neat and tidy.

"Steph! You're here already." Melinda stands to greet her.

I lean over to Candice and whisper, "I thought that in the military, you couldn't hug or anything. They seem pretty informal for military rank personnel."

Before Candice can answer, Melinda jumps in. "While we are military, I keep everything informal because we are a small group. Counting Steph, we have a total staff of eight."

"Where are the other five?" Candice asks.

"They work within our office. Researching and more administrative stuff."

"You said to be here at 2:30 on the dot," Stephanie says, returning to the previous statement about her punctuality. She turns an appraising eye on me. "It's a pleasure to meet you, finally."

"Melinda told me that you're designing a costume for my trip?" I ask.

"That's correct, I have it built, I just need to get you fitted." Stephanie turns to Melinda. "Is it okay if I steal these girls away from you?"

Stephanie leads us down the hallway to another large room, this one filled with Hollywood-style vanities and fitted with a Vegas amount of lighting. She gives us the grand tour, showing us a series of closets stuffed with shoes, shirts, and even evening gowns.

Candice and I are in awe.

"If you think that is cool, wait until you see this!" Stephanie flicks a light switch on the wall. A panel drops open on the wall, revealing shelves that display the most beautiful jewelry I've ever seen.

As I move closer, I see dozens of diamond necklaces of all difference shapes and sizes. One that draws my attention immediately is the rounded emerald and diamond design. I bet that it must weigh a lot.

"Is... Is... this real?" I ask.

"There are no real items here. This is prop jewelry. I have to plan for any mission, so when I see a piece on display that I believe would work in the field, I get the measurements and have a paste copy made," she says.

"Don't you have to worry about theft?" Candice asks.

"No, we have the best security here at the base." Stephanie picks up one of the numerous prop diamond necklaces. "Jackie, here's the necklace you'll be wearing tomorrow."

"Why do I need to wear jewelry?" I hesitated.

She slips it around my neck and fastens the latch. "I was advised by Melinda to make sure every detail was meticulous and correct when it comes to a mission."

"So, in other words, like a movie set?" I state.

"This necklace was created based off of a piece worn by many First Ladies on special events. It was stolen from the White House in 1953 by a former employee and sent to the White House vault after the trial."

While we all admire the necklace, I spot a red thing out of the corner of my eye.

"Is that my dress for tomorrow?" She walks over and grabs it off the rack. It's still wrapped in dry cleaning plastic. She tears that off and brings it over.

"This is an outfit that I designed myself. It is a replica of a dress from the late 1960s. I just have to make sure it fits. I had photos of you from Facebook to use as a reference. So, we'll see if I guessed right."

I'm so excited, I start peeling off my clothes right away. Stephanie slips the dress off the hanger. "It has a zipper all the way down the back."

Before she can put the dress on, I ask about the wetsuit. She explains that the dress has the matching jacket with the built-in flotation devices and the stocking tights are a shade or two darker than my skin tone. They feel soft, though, I am skeptical on how they will hold up.

I unzip the back and step into the dress. It's so soft I could sleep in it. "Candice, will you zip me up?"

She does, and we all admire the effect in the full-length mirror. "Did you sew some kind of magic into this thing?" I ask Stephanie. "I look so skinny!" The outfit, carmine red, is a skirt suit with a matching blazer, all in an exciting, ribbed pattern. The shell top has a tapered waist. The blazer top has a rounded hem, petite lapels, and matching buttons.

"I had a slimmer sewn into it to give you curvy features. I thought you might like that." She rummages in a closet and brings out a pair of sky-high heels.

I haven't worn heels in twenty years. Even at the Gala last year, I wore a long gown with sneakers. "Do I really have to wear these heels?" I ask.

"No, I just wanted to scare you," she giggled, and she selected another pair. "These are heels but more durable and not so high. Have you seen these before?" Stephanie asks.

"Not in a few decades," I say, looking at the new pair. These match the dress color and are stocky. The heel is wide and supportive. The toe box is curved but wide. I slip into them and see how they feel. I hold onto Candice with one arm while Stephanie slips my right foot in.

"Wow! What are these made of? They have so much cushion." I turn to Candice. "You gotta try these on."

Stephanie hands her another pair of heels. "Size 8, right?"

"How did you know?" Candice accepts the pair of heels to try on and moves to a bench by the wall. She kicks off her sneakers and slides into the left shoe first. "Wow! It's a perfect fit."

She stands for a moment and walks a few steps. "How do they feel?" Stephanie asks.

Candice does a small twirl and responds, "Like a brand-new pair of tennis shoes. They're so comfortable. Can I buy these from you?"

"Sure, they are about $2000 a pair," Stephanie giggles.

"How did you ever come across such a comfortable pair of shoes?" I ask.

"Well, I needed something that agents in the field could wear for days at a time. So, I worked with the Defense Secretary's uniform director, and together we invented these comfortable heels." Stephanie nods at my sister. "When you are finished being a princess, put them back on the shelf. Jackie, let's get you a wig."

My eyes open wide. "Wig?" I've never worn a wig in my life. What kind of wig?"

Stephanie pulls a box from the table beside her and opens it. Out pops a dark brown wig, in a retro bob style. "This way, you'll fit in with the early seventies fashion," she remarks.

"Won't the wig get lost in the water?" Candice questions.

"Yes, it will. But by then the mission will be over, and it won't matter."

Candice smirks. "Does that apply for the shoes?"

Stephanie frowns and denies Candice's request. We try on a few more outfits, but the red dress is by far the best one. I'm in love with it. Stephanie agrees and puts my wig back into the box.

"Well, ladies, I'll get to work on some last minor details," Stephanie says. "I'll see you tomorrow for the mission fitting."

I slip back into the clothes I was wearing earlier, and Stephanie walks us back to the conference room.

Agent Taylor is waiting for us. I hope he had a crossword puzzle or something. "Agent Taylor," Stephanie greets him. "Thank you for waiting. I have all the measurements I need. The garments will be ready by 0700 tomorrow." Stephanie waves at us before closing the door behind her.

"Where's Melinda?" Candice asks.

"She was called to the White House for a briefing. But she asked me to set you both up in a hotel tonight," Agent Taylor said.

"Hotel? You said we'd be going home," I protest.

"Yes, that was the plan, but Melinda didn't think you would agree so soon. We've arranged for you to stay at the Holiday Travel Resort next to the base."

CHAPTER 5

We gather our belongings and follow Agent Taylor to the SUV, and he drives us to the hotel just on the other side of the base.

The hotel is very opulent, with four marble columns acting as the grand entrance to the lobby. A bellhop in a dark maroon uniform with gold lettering opens our door and helps us to the front desk. Since we don't have any baggage, we must be his easiest customers of the night. I give him a ten-dollar tip for his courtesy.

The lobby is filled with elegant and rich wood furniture on top of Persian rugs. Below, the marble floor covers the vast lobby and into the hallways. When I think of the money this hotel must have cost to build, I get a headache. The rich like their expensive oases. Judging by the number of luxury cars out in front, the hotel owners are rolling in money.

Candice and I walk up to the front desk, not sure what we're supposed to do or say. The hotel at home is way less intimidating than this huge facility. Mrs. Winterling wouldn't know where to start if she had to run this place.

An impeccably groomed woman looks up from behind the imposing marble counter. "Hello, how may I help you this evening?"

"Checking in for Jackie Jette," I say. I hand her my photo ID.

She accepts my ID and types my name into her computer. Candice and I take a minute to look around the hotel lobby. There's a Grecian statue that rises in the center of the room and is surrounded by a water fountain on all sides. The walls are lined with similar statues but not as grand, obviously, so as not to take away from the center attraction. Around the fountain are small lounge tables with a chair on both sides. I look up and see that the ceiling is crested with golden leaves and more

Grecian designs. Taking a moment to admire the beauty, the employee behind the desk breaks our stares.

"Alright, ladies, here are your room keys. I have you in room 6063 which is on Level 6. Exit the elevators, turn right and just down the hall."

The woman points in the direction of the elevators and we take our keys and thank her. While we wait for the elevator to reach the lobby floor, I turn to Candice. "Wow, this hotel is the finest establishment that I have ever seen."

"I am speechless at the sheer beauty. Every corner has a unique detail," Candice gleamed.

Room 6063 turns out to be an enormous suite with the same marble floor, cold to the touch when I slip off my sneakers. There are two queen beds, covered with a bleach white comforter tucked into the sides. In front of the window is a living space with two chairs that match the ones from the lobby and a small table. Candice races over to the window and whips the curtains open to see the skyline of the city.

Once we settle in, I decide to take a shower. Entering the bathroom, I feel my jaw lower at the sight of the large jacuzzi tub and shower combo. There is no shower curtain. Instead, there are glass doors that surround the top of the tub wall and extend up to the ceiling.

Now relaxed in the hot water, steam rises above me. The best thing about the glass wall is the steam stays isolated, creating a spa like feel. I am rocked from my spa day when I hear two knocks at the bathroom door.

"Jackie, if I order room service, do you want anything?"

I think for a moment about my food choices. Dinnertime passed a while ago, but this hotel kitchen is open 24/7 according to the sign at the hotel front desk. The had an advertisement for their full line of desserts hanging in the elevator. Of course, dessert sounded better than dinner to me.

"What do they have?" I ask.

"If you would stop soaking in the tub and come out here, you could see what they have."

Sad to leave this luxury tub, I pull the drain plug and dry myself with the large white cotton towel. Wrapping the towel around my body and letting my hair go curly, I exit the bathroom, navigating my way to the chair where Candice is sitting. She hands me the menu.

"Everything sounds so delicious. I am going to order the shrimp fettuccini," I say. "What are you craving?"

"I want the chicken Caesar salad," Candice remarks, and I am curious as to why she is ordering a salad. When she places the order with the representative from the kitchen, she adds on two slices of brownie bottom cheesecake.

"I knew that you had an agenda when you ordered a salad," I heckled.

The food arrives within thirty minutes via a white-linen-covered service cart. The server, a man in a uniform similar to the bellhop but with colors reversed, in a brilliant shade of gold with maroon lettering, brought the cart in and removed the covers. Our mouths became a tidal wave of cravings.

As soon as he left the room, we dive in. The shrimp is delicious, and there is not a drop of sauce left on my plate thanks to the bread that came on the side. Candice finishes off her salad, which could have fed two people. Devouring the dessert is easy. The chocolate is rich and the brownie bottom crust so soft that it melts in our mouths, still warm.

By the time our dessert plates are cleaned, Candice and I are stuffed and ready for bed. I place the used dinnerware and cutlery outside of the door and lock the door up. A trick I learned — again, from my aunt Jess — is to take three to four clothes hangers and place them between the door and the latch for extra security.

We both fall asleep from pure exhaustion. The day's events were tiresome, but tomorrow the adventure *really* begins.

CHAPTER 6

After a restful sleep, we head down for breakfast at the hotel restaurant. The five-star breakfast is complimentary, so Candice and I jump at the chance. We don't get the royal treatment like this in Bluefin Cove.

We head right for the buffet line, filling our plates with scrambled eggs, country potatoes, bacon and bread pudding. Then we arrive at the end of the line, which has three large beverage dispensers, one with water and the others with orange juice and coffee. I choose coffee to caffeinate myself while Candice chooses orange juice. With our hands full, we find an empty table and plant our roots.

"*Ugggh,* this is so delicious!" I groan. "Candice, what's your favorite part?"

"Oh, the bacon! A hundred percent!" she replies, gobbling up her fourth slice.

My phone pings with a text message from Agent Taylor. I read it out to Candice. "Good morning. I'll be waiting for you by the lobby door at 10 a.m."

Candice looks at her wristwatch. "Jackie, it's a quarter to ten now. We better head out to the lobby."

I tuck a twenty-dollar bill under the saltshaker for the servers. "Ready?" I say, and we get up to go. Candice's phone chimes as we walk out of the restaurant. She pulls out her phone and checks it. "It's from Grace. She said the shop is running smoothly, and she'll deliver the Bowling League florals after closing."

That's a relief. The Bowling League gala is the biggest floral arrangement of the year. Since Candice bought the shop, sales have just gone up and up. The lady who owned it before only opened in the spring and summer. Now, Candice — with a little help from her big sister — has created a year-round shop, selling floral arrangements for every occasion.

While Candice takes a minute to call Grace, I duck into the hotel gift shop. I want to look for a souvenir to take home, and sure enough I find a cute little snow globe with a miniature Air Force One inside. I purchase it immediately.

Shopping is always my defense when I am stressed or nervous about something. Back in Bluefin Cove, in our den, we have a wall with the surviving snow globes that Dad picked up for us on his many trips. A few of oldest globes are yellow on the inside, and some have lost their shine, but the memory will never fade. Since I am starting this role, I want to have something to remember it by.

When I get outside, Candice is waving frantically at me. "It's 9:58!" We speed walk to the lobby, where Agent Taylor is waiting.

Back in the SUV, we buckle up and speed away from the hotel toward the base. The city is so beautiful. It's nothing like postcards or pictures online. The amount of greenery is astonishing. I notice that the larger trees are swaying back and forth as if they are in the middle of a slow dance. The squirrels are on the hunt for food, climbing up and down the tree trunks. *Oh, there's one flying to the neighboring tree.*

When we get to the base, Agent Taylor lowers his window and displays his badge. The guards open the gates, and we drive on through. My heart is pounding with adrenaline. He takes us to the hangar, where Melinda and Stephanie are waiting to greet us with fresh coffee.

Melinda passes folders out to each of us, then she begins to brief us on the game plan for the day. "All right, everyone, thank you for being here. We have a lot to go over before we attempt to send Jackie to 1971."

When she says it out loud, my heart beats even faster. I squeeze my sister's hand under the table. *Are we really doing this?*

Melinda continues our briefing. "We have a piece of the lavatory mirror. Now, we don't know which mirror it is. You could end up forward or aft of the aircraft as they are the identical part numbers. After Stephanie gets you dressed, you'll walk with us to the secondary hangar, we'll give you the mirror fragment, and we'll see what happens. If you turn to page 4, you'll see a diagram of the Boeing 707 similar to your dad's airplane. I want you to memorize it. The lavatory is your access point."

"What do I do once on board?" I ask her. "*If* I manage to travel back in time, that is."

"Once on board, it's absolutely crucial that you keep an eye on the time. In a few moments, we'll listen to the crash tapes that have been recovered from the seafloor. We know the exact moment the recording stops. You must touch the lavatory mirror before that time to be safe."

"But what am I looking for during my time there?"

"Talk to the crew, observe the cabin and its passengers. You are not to talk to your dad. He has no idea what's going to happen."

"Can I even say hello?" I ask, but Melinda shakes her head.

"Absolutely not," she repeats. "If you lose track of time, the consequences could be catastrophic. Now, Jackie, at any moment if you feel like it's time to return to present day, you head for the lavatory that you arrived in and touch that mirror. Let's not take any chances," Melinda remarks.

Once Melinda is satisfied, Stephanie takes me to her office to get changed. I slip into the custom-made outfit, and she zips me up and adjusts it.

She then has me sit in a barber chair for my wig fitting. She places a wig cap over my hair, then slides the wig on and secures it with bobby pins. The mirror in front of me displays my new look. Going from curly dirty blonde hair to a dark brown bob is quite a change.

Stephanie does my makeup, finishing with a generous amount of hairspray. Then she kneels and inserts my feet into the red heels.

Once my shoes are snug, Stephanie escorts me to a low table, where all my equipment is laid out. "There's a number of items that are important to your trip," Stephanie explains. "First, there's a radio beacon in your dress that will sound when you enter salt water. As Melinda said in the briefing earlier, a Navy ship will be standing by in the Atlantic, waiting for you. Also, the top button on your dress doubles as light for the ship to see you. It will last for six hours on the small battery inside. Only water will activate it. Next, there's your purse. Before you press the lavatory mirror, make sure your purse is sealed shut. That way the items inside will be protected from the water."

She opens the purse and shows me the waterproof camera inside, explaining how to use it. When I press it twice, the camera will take twenty photos in five seconds.

The next item she pulls out is a passport. "Should you get picked up by anyone else other than the US Navy, show them the last page in your passport."

I turn to the last page and see a series of numbers. "What do all of these bold numbers mean?" I pointed to the spot.

"The number is the same one as your government ID number, and it follows within the Geneva Convention."

"What is the Geneva Convention again?" Candice asks, as I couldn't remember what the rules or purpose was since we learned it in high school a few decades ago.

"The Geneva Convention, specifically the 159 articles of the Fourth Geneva Convention, apply to your trip. Should you be captured by a foreign country's armed forces, you are protected from torture or brutality or discrimination," Agent Taylor explained. "Does that make it easier to understand?"

We nod our heads, and I dive back into the purse. Other items inside the bag consist of a lipstick, ticket jacket, tourist flyers, and cigarettes. Typical items that a person traveling to Rome would have.

"That's all that I have for you. Do you have any more questions about your uniform?" Stephanie asks.

I shake my head, then face the three-pane mirror, admiring myself again. Stephanie snaps a few photos of my getup.

"What was that for?" I ask.

"I want to have this for your file. If anything should happen down the road, I know we can recreate this look from the photo. I'll detail all your makeup and equipment, as well."

She leads me back to the conference room. No matter how much these shoes feel like sneakers, my leg still wobbles from the lack of experience in heels. Stephanie has to steady me by the elbow a couple of times. I teeter into the room, and everyone falls silent.

"Wow! You deserve a Nobel Prize for miracles!" Candice tells Stephanie.

"Stephanie's a very talented asset," Melinda smiles. "Do a little twirl for me, please." I do as she says, and I haven't felt like a girl in so many years. It's nice to be a girly-girl once in a while.

"Can Jackie borrow that dress if she ever gets a date?" Candice wants to know. We all laugh, since everyone knows I've been single for years.

"I don't have time for romance, Candice." I tell her. "I'm too busy time-traveling. At least, I *think* I am."

We all take our seats. "Before we head over to the hangar," Melinda says, "I wanted to have you listen to the cockpit voice recorder. Pay attention, and remember as much as possible. That way, when you're in 1971, you'll know what's about to happen."

Melinda pulls out her phone and starts the recording. There's a visual that accompanies it, showing the current time in 1971. And for the first time in half a century, I hear my father's voice.

18:45:02

"Good evening, ladies and gentlemen, this is Captain Jette speaking. We're cruising at our assigned altitude of 32,000 feet, and our ground speed is 502 miles an hour. Our estimated time of arrival is just after 1 a.m. local time. If you need anything, please let a flight attendant know. Thank you for choosing Americonic, and enjoy the flight."

18:45:58

"Gentlemen? Would you all like some coffee?"

18:46:04

[inaudible chatter]

18:46:52

"Three coffees, all black. Coming up. Here's the menu for dinner tonight. I'll be back with coffee and to grab your orders."

18:49:00

"Americonic 329, Boston Center copy."

18:49:05

"Boston Center, Americonic 329, go ahead."

18:49:13

"Americonic 329, Boston Center, pilots reporting turbulence, please climb to 370 and maintain."

18:49:28

"Boston Center, Americonic 329, roger, climb and maintain 370 for turbulence."

18:49:35

"Dan, go ahead and take us up to 370."

18:49:59

[dials clicking, engine noise increase]

18:50:30

"Gentlemen, I'm going to stretch my legs. Dan, it's your aircraft."

18:50:55

"My aircraft." [sound of cockpit door opening and closing]

18:55:00

"Boston Center, Americonic 329, copy."

18:55:10

"Americonic 329, Boston Center. Go ahead, Americonic 329."

18:55:17

"Boston Center, Americonic 329. We are maintaining flight level 370."

18:56:24

"Roger Americonic 329. Please maintain level 370 until further notice."

19:01:56

We sit in silence. "Dad's voice…" I finally say. "I'd forgotten what it sounded like."

Candice has tears rolling down her face.

"He seemed so relaxed and happy," she says.

"He had no idea what was coming for him." Melinda remarks. "The best thing that we can do for him now is find out what happened when the recording stopped."

She rolls back the tape and enhances the audio, playing the last three seconds at the end. "If you listen closely, you can hear a small bang." Melinda says and then plays the tape. We listen very closely, and sure enough the bang is there.

Agent Taylor jumps in. "It had to be something quiet in the front of the aircraft or something louder in the rear of the aircraft."

We turn our heads back to Melinda after Agent Taylor finishes his statement. "We have no proof of conversations or continued flight after the audio tape ends. That is what we have to find out."

"There's no way to decipher what happened in the passenger cabin specifically?" Candice asks.

Melinda shakes her head. "No ma'am. Back in 1971, these devices were revolutionary. I'm just glad that this much has survived."

"Do you or your team have an idea as to what could have caused the bang?" I ask.

"We can speculate all day long, but that is just what it is: speculation. That's why we need you to help us find out what happened."

My stomach is tying itself in knots. I want to chicken out so badly, but I also want to do this for my dad and for Candice. We've been wondering for the past fifty years what happened.

Melinda interrupts my train of thought. "It's time." We exit the building and pile into Agent Taylor's car. He takes us to another hangar at the airfield, leading us to a room that says AUTHORIZED ACCESS ONLY. There's a security panel to the right of the door. Melinda swipes a badge and enters a key code.

"Damn," mutters Agent Taylor. "*I* don't even have that code."

"And you won't get it," Melinda quips back, as she pushes open the heavy metal door. Inside, the room looks like a bank safety deposit box vault. There are hundreds of little locked drawers lining the walls.

"What *is* this place?" Candice asks. Ignoring her, Melinda locates a box in the middle of the far wall and opens the panel. She slides the heavy box out and motions to us to approach.

"Each drawer contains a piece of wreckage from a crash that your dad investigated. I've been adding pieces, over the years. One day, as soon as orders permitted, we knew that we would be able to resume this operation — and here you are." Melinda places the box on a table at the center of the room.

From it, she lifts out a small, shiny object. "Is that the mirror?" I ask. "How do you know it's not from a makeup compact, or some other thing?"

"We thought of that. See the corner here? Those last five digits match the original part number from the manufacturer, Boeing. Their engineers confirmed that it's a piece of the lavatory mirror, but based on the aircraft maintenance logs, part number D87D26730-113 was registered in the forward lavatory. Let's hope that the logs are correct."

"That's reassuring," I say. "Do I just touch it and see what happens?"

"Yup, that's about the size of it," Agent Taylor replies.

"I wish it was more scientific than that, but Agent Taylor's right," Melinda explains. "Do you want to say anything before you try it?"

"Um, yeah. Candice, if I don't return, go see Ed back home. He has my will."

Then I grab her and hug her tight.

I think of how much our lives have changed since yesterday morning when I was sitting in the Bluefin Café, drinking my coffee and watching people surf. *Now I'm about to time travel. Candice found out she's adopted and was born in 1953. After I touch this thing, our lives could change forever.*

Candice breaks the hug first, wiping at the corners of her eyes.

"You'll be back," she tells me. "You're too damn stubborn to get lost out there." We hug again and she says, "I love you, sis." Finally, we let go.

"Are you ready?" Agent Taylor asks me.

"Yes. Let's see if I have the gift." Melinda moves the mirror fragment closer to me.

Agent Taylor smiles encouragingly. "Good luck, Jackie."

I look at Candice one last time before reaching out and touching the mirror.

Everything goes dark. I have no idea where or when I am.

I peer through the dark, trying to get my bearings. I reach out and feel a wall, then a ceiling, then another wall. I run my hands along the wall looking for some type of handle, doorknob, or light switch.

There's a humming noise, and a vibration in the walls. *It smells weird in here.* Like an industrial air freshener, mixed with old cigarette smoke.

There's a bump on the wall. It's a handle of some sort. I wiggle it around and it pops to the right. Moments later I see a flicker of light.

I look at my reflection in the mirror. I am still wearing the same red dress and wig. There's a toilet, towel dispenser and a feminine hygiene kit below the towels.

I'm in the lavatory. I did it! I time-traveled.

I start to have a panic attack. My breathing comes fast and hard, and I let out a whimper. There's a knock on the door and a female voice says, "Ma'am? Are you okay? Do you need assistance?"

Get it together, Jackie. "No, thank you. I'm okay. I just... ahh... slipped, but it's all good now." I force myself to focus. Looking at my wristwatch, I see that it's 18:42. *I have 18 minutes until the bang.*

CHAPTER 7

Present day, In Melinda's office with Agent Taylor.

"It worked?" Candice shouts to Melinda and Agent Taylor. "She just vanished!"

The small mirror fragment that Jackie touched is still sitting on the table. There's a single fingerprint on it.

"Wow, it was just like the reports and stories from my previous boss, Ken." Melinda's just as stunned as Candice, since this was a first for her too.

"She did it. My gosh, she did it!" Agent Taylor looks thrilled.

Candice looks forlornly at the two officials. "What do we do now?" she asks as tears streak down her cheeks.

Melinda notices how upset Candice is and walks over to her, wrapping her arms around Candice's shoulders. "May I offer a few wise words that provided me with a giggle during the tough challenges?" Candice nods as she could use the laughter. "Attention, Kmart shoppers." Both of them chuckle and Melinda uses a tissue from the desk to wipe away Candice's tears.

Melinda suggests. "How about we return to my office and go over your file as a distraction?"

Candice had forgotten about the file with all of the excitement around the time travel. But she still hesitates. "Do we need to do anything for Jackie's return?" she asks.

Melinda shakes her head. "The USS Lavon is already in position, waiting for Jackie."

"Why is the ship already in position?" Candice questioned. "How did you know that Jackie would do it?"

"I didn't know, but I wanted to be prepared, and the ship was already in the area assisting with the wreck salvage operation." Melinda states.

At that, Candice feels a measure of comfort, and Agent Taylor drives them back to the first hangar, where Melinda has the files on Candice's birth family.

"I'm going to work in my office for a little bit," Agent Taylor tells them. "If you need anything, just let me know." Melinda nods, steering Candice toward her office.

"Would you like another cup of coffee?" she asks. "We may be awake for a long time while we wait for your sister."

"Do you have any tea?" Candice asks.

"See, you *do* have English roots," Melinda smiles.

Melinda sits in her leather office chair while Candice takes a seat on the opposite side of her desk. Reaching into the file drawer by her desk, Melinda digs for a moment and then retrieves the blue file. She turns the front cover and reveals the first page.

"Right on the top is your original birth certificate." Melinda looks up at Candice. "You saw this one yesterday, right?" Candice nods and then Melinda pulls out a second document. "This is the investigation report from your birth parents' plane crash. I know it's difficult to read. Would you like me to read it to you?"

With a shaky voice, Candice concedes. "Yes, that would be great."

"Okay, I'll start here. If you have a question, feel free to stop me." Sliding on her reading glasses, she begins to read:

"On January 1, 1954, Royal Overseas Airways Flight 15 took off from Rome destined for London. The aircraft climbed to 27,000 feet, and the captain was in contact until 10:51am. At that time, it was believed that the aircraft experienced a sudden decompression and crashed into a field on the island of Elba. According to the rescue personnel, no survivors were found as the accident was deemed not survivable."

Candice interrupted, "If the crash was deemed unsurvivable, how did he save me?"

Melinda read down the paper to the notes on the bottom written by Ken and said, "Your dad was on the aircraft for only a few moments before it broke apart. He was able grab you and time travel just before the explosive decompression happened." Melinda answers.

"So, I was ripped away from my parents?" Candice asks.

Melinda said, "According to documentation based on your dad's version of the event, you mom somehow found out who Paul was, and she begged him to take you. Against orders, Paul accepted."

Candice begins to tear up. "Please continue."

"The next part is more descriptive, and I want to advise you of that."

"That's okay," Candice whispers. "I need to know."

"Initial examination of the aircraft wreckage revealed several signs that the airplane broke up mid-air. Pieces of cabin flooring were found stuck in the remains of the tail section; the imprint of an American coin was found on a fuselage panel from the rear of the aircraft; and smears and scoring on the rear fuselage were tested and found to be consistent with the paint applied to the passenger seats that were a match for maintenance records of the aircraft. When most of the wreckage was recovered, investigators discovered that fractures started in the roof, a window then broke away and rammed into the back elevators, the back fuselage then tore away, the outer wing structure broke away after failing, then the outer wing tips and finally the cockpit broke away and fuel from the wings set the debris on fire."

"What happened to my parents?" Candice asks. "Did they find any… remains?"

Melinda sets the paper down and digs back into the file. After sifting through a few pages, she removes two documents. "These are the death certificates," she says. "But the photos are too graphic to show you; plus, they're located in a different file. I do have a photograph from when they were in Rome with you. Would you like to see it?"

"Yes!" Candice shouts, then catches herself. "I mean, yes please."

Melinda digs in the file again and removes the photo, handing it to Candice. It's a black and white photo of a couple sitting at a table on a cobblestone street. The woman wears an elegant 1950s dress, and the man is wearing a traditional suit. In between the couple is a baby stroller, an infant sleeping within.

"This is the very last photo of you and your birth parents. The next morning, they would perish in the crash. We found this same baby stroller in the wreckage as well as your parents' suitcase."

Astonished that their suitcase would survive such a horrible disaster, Candice questions Melinda, "Their suitcase was still intact?"

"Yes, Ken located the suitcase from an underground warehouse in 1971 once your father returned with you. Investigators identified the luggage as your parents based on the bag tag still attached."

Candice asked, "Wouldn't the impact of the crash destroy the suitcase or at least burn it?"

"When the airplane broke apart in the sky, many items were scattered across a few square miles. Would you like to see it?" Melinda asked, but she already knew that Candice would want to see it. She leans forward and presses the intercom. "Sally, will you please bring in the suitcase that we discussed earlier?"

"Who is Sally?" Candice solicited.

"She is my assistant. Her office is just through those doors there." Melinda pointed.

Turning back to the photo, Candice asks "May I have this photo? I mean, I know it's evidence, but--"

"Candice, you may have anything in this file that you wish," Melinda tells her. "The only reason we kept these items for so long was for you once our orders were lifted. You may have the photo and also the suitcase."

Candice takes a moment to wipe her tears. Moments later, Sally bursts through the doors with suitcase on a trolley. She places the suitcase on the table for closer examination, then exits.

"Candice, come on over," Melinda says.

Candice stands, studying the brown leather case. It looks like a steamer trunk, but it's not as large. She touches the destination tag that has somehow remained on the front handle even after the crash. It displays a city destination code of EGCR. "What city is that?" Candice asks.

"London," Melinda says. "London Croydon Airport."

"I've never heard of that destination before," Candice interjects.

Melinda affirms, "Croydon was the major international airport before London Heathrow was built. Now, Croydon is more of a museum."

Candice flips over the tag. "Charles Carter," she reads. "Was that his name?" she asks. "Charles?"

"Yes," Melinda confirms, scanning the birth certificate. "And here's a side note. Your parents were married on November 23, 1953. You were born the next July, so Christine must have been pregnant already. Now," she continues gently, "would you like to open the case and see what's inside?"

"What's inside? Have you seen the contents yet?"

Melinda mumbled. "While I have had the curious urge to sneak a peek of the contents, Ken gave me strict orders not to open it until this day. Otherwise, it stayed in a secured location."

Candice nods her head and unlatches the buckles, first the one on the left and then the one on the right. The case creaks open despite the damage from a 27,000-foot drop to the ground below.

The top layer is an assortment of undergarments, both men's and women's. There are a few cloth baby diapers with the fasteners. A few pairs of trousers lay under those. Candice digs around the clothing and stumbles upon a nearly full bottle of women's perfume.

On closer examination, Candice can read a faint name etched on the glass. She tries to sound it out but Melinda takes it from her. "It's from Europe. It's called *Rose d'enchantement..*

Candice takes the bottle, squeezing the puffer. A small mist of fragrance sprays from the bottle and Candice inhales the smell. It's a spiced scent of bergamot, cedarwood and roses.

"Elegant," Melinda comments. "Your birth mother had taste."

Candice places the bottle to the side and continues through the items. The next thing that catches her eye is a baby blanket with pinkish embroidery—a little yellowed from time--that reads "Our little princess, beautiful and humble, fear not as sorrow allows a path forward." The words are surrounded by two angels, embroidered in gold and silver. Candice lifts the small blanket to her nose and inhales, but all she can smell is mildew.

There are trousers, undergarments, makeup, and a few souvenirs. On the bottom of the case are two dresses. Candice holds them up, recognizing one from the photo that Melinda gave her.

She holds it up to her neck and admires the design. It's printed with a scattering of pink and red roses. The other dress has a similar design but with blue and green flowers.

Melinda has an idea. "If you want, when we finish, I can have Stephanie help you try these on?"

Candice grew concerned. "I don't want to tear or damage the dress. After all of these years, won't it be brittle?"

"If anyone can treat a garment with care, it's Stephanie." Melinda says confidently.

Worried that she is taking Melinda from her duties, Candice shakes her head. "Melinda, you're already doing so much for me. I don't want to impose."

"You and you sister are doing a lot for the world today. Plus, I work on a base with mostly men, so it's nice to have girl time."

Candice starts crying again and grabs a tissue from the dispenser on the desk. She wipes away her tears and then lays the dresses down on the chair back behind her.

The next item Candice lifts from the suitcase is a jewelry box. The logo reads Pearl-Norms Jewelry, London.

Candice strains to open the box, though the hinges are badly corroded. Eventually the lid comes loose, and the box opens to reveal a magnificent pearl necklace with matching earrings.

Candice holds the pearls up and admires them. "Why wouldn't she wear these every day? I'd never take them off."

"Well, she was wearing a different diamond necklace on the day of the crash, as the autopsy photos revealed. British officials buried her with the necklace she was wearing."

Aside from the dresses, jewelry and makeup, Candice's father's suit jackets are folded inside, as well as his shaving kit. The kit contains a razor, mustache cream and a shattered bottle of aftershave.

Candice reaches the bottom of the suitcase where a bundle of baby clothes lies. Then she carefully repacks the items.

"Thank you for keeping this for me. You have no idea how much it means," Candice says. "I can't wait to tell my sister about it."

"It's my pleasure, Candice. Do you want to take the dresses down the hall and try them on?" Melinda asks.

"Absolutely!" Candice grabs the dresses from the chair back, and the two women march to Stephanie's workshop.

Melinda knocks on the office door. A moment later, Stephanie opens the doors with a mouth full of food. She waves them in and points to the large armchairs in front of her desk and they take a seat. "Sorry about that!" she swallows. "What can I do for you, ladies?"

Melinda indicates the two dresses. "Will you please help Candice try these on and see if they fit?"

Stephanie inspects the dresses. "Wait! Are these the dresses from her birth mother's suitcase?"

"Mm-hm!" Melinda nods.

"How did you know about them?" Candice challenged.

Stephanie ignored the question grabbing the frocks from Melinda. "Hmm," she says. "There's some damage here, and they both are in need of a new lining."

"Do you have any spare lining in the back?" Melinda points toward the supply closet.

"Mhmm. I think I have enough to fix one dress. I will have to dig around in the back," she says.

Candice looks crestfallen, but Stephanie runs around the corner and rolls out a Singer sewing machine on wheels. "Don't worry!" she insists. "After seventy years, it would be weird if they *weren't* damaged. I'll take care of it, Candice. Pull up a chair and talk while I work on this."

Melinda and Candice sit around Stephanie as she deconstructs damaged sections and adds a new zipper to the back of one dress. Candice takes a moment to learn more about Melinda.

"If I may, and I don't mean any offense, but for being a military department, the atmosphere around your office and staff seems —"

Melinda finishes her sentence. "Informal? Relaxed?"

"Well," Candice clears her throat, hoping not to offend. "Yes. I thought that the government agents would all be like Agent Taylor. Formal and uptight."

"Agent Taylor is the most *uptight* agent here. The rest of us were simple civilian contractors at one time," Melinda expresses.

"When did that change?" Candice asks.

"In late 1996, Ken decided that he was near retirement. He pulled me into a meeting first thing on a Monday morning. May 20 to be exact; I still remember it to this day. He advised me that of all the people that he had managed, I was his first choice with confidential information."

Candice jumps in. "Wow, that had to be a big surprise."

"It truly was a surprise but also suspicious at the same time," she warns.

"What do you mean?" Candice questions, with an eyebrow raised.

"Ken was always like a father figure to me at the office, and for him to bring me in for an unplanned meeting was a trembling experience. The conclusion of our meeting resulted in Ken retiring and me stepping up to fill his shoes. I still remember the exact words he said. 'Melinda, of all the challenges you face in your career, the Paul Jette case is the most important.' His retirement began in 1997."

Impressed with the story, Candice changes the conversation topic to the discovery of wreckage a few days ago. "What happened when the wreckage was located?"

Melinda beams at the question. "I know finding the wreckage may have been difficult for you and Jackie as well as the families of other passengers who were on board, but when I received the call from a navy vessel via a secured telephone line, I jumped out of my chair. Finding the wreckage meant that I could commence *Operation Bluefin.*"

"That is what this operation was named? Operation Bluefin?" Candice grins.

"Since your mother moved the entire family up to Bluefin Cove, Ken took away the number after operation and changed it to Bluefin. I liked it a lot more."

Melinda and Candice continue to talk about her life leading up to this moment. Melinda shares that she has no kids as her husband, Juan, is unable to father children. He is a retired Air Force One pilot who flew many of the finest presidents when the current plane was unveiled and first put into service. Now he enjoys the retired life and speaking at Veterans' medical clinics to be a friend to those in need.

They are interrupted. "Okay, almost done." Stephanie says as she finishes up the last hem. "And finished!" She stands from the machine and says, "Come on, girls, over here in front of the mirror."

Candice and Melinda follow, and Candice gets out of her shirt and pants. She slips on the pink and red flower dress and Stephanie zips it up. A little adjustment here and a little there. Stephanie pins the spots where she needs to take it in. A few seams pop in the process but Stephanie reassures Candice that she can repair them.

Candice stands there in silence. After a few moments, she breathes, "Wow, my mother's dress is so beautiful. They don't make them like this anymore."

"I beg to differ!" Stephanie says, slightly offended.

Melinda giggles. "Well, no one but you, Stephanie."

Stephanie walks over to the table and picks up the other dress. Bringing it to Candice, she says, "Let's see you in this one."

Melinda hops up and unzips Candice so that she can slip into the blue one. Once the dress is off, Melinda inserts a hanger to prevent the pins from falling out and hangs it on the coat rack in the corner.

Candice shimmies the blue dress up to her shoulders. "Wow, your mother must have bought this from the same dressmaker around the same time." Stephanie zips up the back.

"Why do you say that?" Melinda asks.

"It's the same thread, the same fine work. It's not by a machine." Stephanie places her pins here and there. "See, the pins are in the same identical places as the other dress."

"How long will this take?" Candice asks.

"A few hours at most." Stephanie glances at the clock on the wall. "Hey, it's nearly 1900 hours; we should order food. What do you guys want?"

"How about Chinese food?" Melinda suggests. "I'll order and have Sally run and grab it. What do we want?"

"How about a little of everything? Or just surprise us!" Candice suggests.

Melinda steps away for a moment to order the food and Stephanie helps Candice take off the dress.

Candice gets dressed again, then takes her seat by Stephanie, watching her work.

Twenty minutes pass, and Melinda returns with the food. "Whoa! How much food did you order?" Candice asks.

"You said a little of everything! Plus, I invited Sally to join us," Melinda says as she sets the bags on an empty table.

Once the food is devoured, Candice asks, "Do you think Jackie is okay?"

Melinda responds, "If she's anything like her dad, I think she'll be just fine."

"I wonder what happening. I would give anything to have a peep hole into that plane right now," Candice says, holding onto the idea of being a fly on the wall and watching the flight unfold. If anything, just to be there to assist her sister.

Candice leans back in her chair and looks towards the ceiling. "Wherever you are, Sis, I hope you get back safe."

CHAPTER 8

Emerging from the lavatory, I step into the cabin, and immediately I'm aware of a constant humming sound mixed with the clinking of porcelain and glassware. Among these noises, I can hear the chatter of voices through the cabin, both male and female.

The forward door and crew jump seats are directly in my path. As I turn to my right, there is a wall with a smaller door in the middle, and in all capital letters it says COCKPIT. Below the letters, there is a peephole. I look to my left and see a white half circular booth with a coffee table in the middle. The table is attached to the wall paneling and allows just enough room to scoot by and take a seat. I decide to plant myself there for a few moments while I gather my thoughts.

The window shades are in the open position, but all I can see is my reflection from the lighting in the cabin. The sky outside is dark. I see no city lights, so we must be over the Atlantic. Two chimes sound from the overhead speaker, followed by a familiar voice.

"Good evening, ladies and gentlemen, this is Captain Jette speaking. We are cruising at our assigned altitude of 32,000 feet, with a ground speed of 502 miles an hour. Our estimated time of arrival is just after 1 a.m. local time. If you need anything, please let a flight attendant know. Thank you for choosing Americonic International, and enjoy the flight."

Once he finishes the announcement, I raise my hand and glance at my watch. The time is 18:46. Which means I only have 16 minutes until the loud bang happens and this beautiful jetliner becomes a worldwide icon on every news network.

The interior is more luxurious than the modern planes I'm used to. I've never seen a commercial airplane with a lounge up front. Magazines are displayed on the tabletop, advertising trips around the world and the latest front page news. I see one that has a political cartoon about war overseas and the word PEACE with a question mark. I leave the magazines alone and focus on my surroundings.

Behind the round booth is a wall that divides the lounge and first class. On the wall is a stunning display of silver birds and airplanes.

The cabin smells of fresh bread; they must be warming rolls for dinner. Drifting my gaze to the left, I can see a room blocked off with a light blue curtain.

A flight attendant pulls back the curtain to reveal a first-class galley behind it. She wears a dark navy blue skirt with a matching jacket and pillbox hat. Her hair is short and curly. As she walks by, I notice how elegantly she carries herself.

"When did you sneak up here?" The young flight attendant says to me in the most admirable British accent.

"Oh, I had to use the bathroom, and I wanted to stretch my legs," I hesitated.

"Ma'am, I have been flying for a few years, and I've got a good memory. I don't recall seeing you in first class when we boarded or completed the safety briefing. Given that your dress stands out, I would have remembered it," she interrogates.

My eyes move away from hers and I look at the name badge pinned on her suit jacket. "Marge?" I state. "I was wearing a different outfit earlier, but I spilt coffee on my blouse. You remember, I said that you had the most beautiful smile when I walked onto the aircraft."

Amused by my remarks, she conceded and apologized for the questioning. Marge continued past me and proceeded to the cockpit door. She was only five steps away from me when a light bulb clicked in my head. Marge is the flight attendant on the recording that spoke to Dad and the other pilots. This means I have 14 minutes and some change before the bang is heard. The dots are starting to connect. Referencing my watch, I see that it is 18:47.

Marge stopping to challenge me resulted in her arriving to ask about coffee nearly two minutes later than on the recording. I am already changing the past.

I refocus as she knocks at the cockpit door, then reaches for the door handle and twists it. I noticed that she's carrying a menu with her. The door closes behind her. *She must be about to take their coffee orders.*

Turning my head away from the front, I peer into the galley through the still-open curtain, where I can see a second flight attendant filling a trolley cart with a variety of beverages and glassware. She notices my stare and stops what she's doing. *Oh no, she's headed my way. I'm in trouble now.*

"Hello ma'am, can I help you with anything?"

I shake my head. "No, thank you. I was just being nosy." She smiles then and returns to her workstation. The first flight attendant exits the cockpit and returns to the galley, busying herself with serving three steaming mugs of fresh coffee.

I know I have a few moments before Dad will come out of the cockpit, so I take this moment to stand and exit the booth. As I travel down the first class aisle, I keep my eye open for anything out of the ordinary. Many of the passengers are focused on their distractions that they brought from home or what they purchased at the airport gift shop. When I walk by, some look up and stare. Considering that I'm dressed in a red outfit with a stunning necklace, they notice me quickly but return to their books, games and other items believing that I am just another passenger.

I smile and examine each passenger, taking note of their physical appearances. I see many of the men wearing suits like they are going to have dinner on Park Avenue or heading for a business meeting, while the women are wearing their best dresses. I see one older lady fixing her makeup and adding a second layer of maroon lipstick. When I get to Row 6 on the port side, I'm shocked to see the TV star Lorraine Reynolds — I had no idea she was on this flight. I watch her reruns all the time at the Bluefin Café. I decide to stop for just a few seconds.

I lean over to be a little more discreet and say, "Hello, Mrs. Reynolds."

"Hi dear!" she responds with a huge smile.

"I know you're busy, but I wanted to say that I love your work and I catch your reruns all the time."

"Reruns?" She asks me in a state of confusion. "My show is still running, darling."

"Oh, you know, when the broadcasting company has to fill unsold space with shows that have —" *think quick, think quick* "— already aired. I just love your show. I'm sorry to have bothered you. Enjoy your flight." I walk away before she can say another word. *Wow, I almost gave myself up.* Even though Melinda said it wouldn't matter who knew me on the plane, the thought of being caught is bothersome.

I reach the rear of the first-class cabin without seeing anything surprising. Proceeding around the curtain divider, I enter the economy section, where the flight attendants are already serving drinks.

Continuing my stroll down the aisle, I pass lots of people playing cards, reading and resting their eyes. I feel my eyes begin to burn at the thought that all these people are going to die in less than twenty minutes. The hardest part of it all is the children. There are no lifeboats to send them into for safety. They are all at the mercy of the universe. I see two children, who appear to be brother and sister, playing a game of checkers on a mini board.

I lean down and smile. "Who's winning?"

The little girl, no older than ten, answers first. "I am. I always win at this game."

"Tia, that is not true. I won a few games while we waited to board in New York."

I giggle, wishing them both good luck. I continue on row by row. At Row 13, I arrive at a second beverage cart.

"Pardon me, so sorry," I say to the attendants as I squeeze past them, careful not to knock over any pitchers or cups. I look down at the cart as I scoot by and notice a difference. The first cart had wine bottles and cocktail mixers, whereas this cart has colas, juices, milks and water. I still don't see anything out of the ordinary.

The cabin is growing narrower as I reach the rear, and I still haven't seen anything abnormal other than a weird ringing in my ears near row 20. Both of the walls at the end of the cabin have a Americonic logo mounted in silver. I see another curtain, lavatories and some doors marked STORAGE. *Maybe the crash is from a structural issue? Or something in the cargo hold? Because there's nothing wrong in the cabin, at least to my eyes.*

I stop by the rear galley, where two more attendants are preparing the ovens for dinner service. They wear white aprons over their navy blue uniforms.

One of the women notices my presence. "Hi ma'am, can I get you anything from the galley, or are you just giving yourself a tour?"

"Oh, I'm just giving myself a tour. It's my first time on this type of airplane. Boy! It's a work of art. We don't have anything like this where I come from," I admit.

She looks confused. "Where do you come from? Do they not have airplanes there?"

"Oh, we have cheap, no-frills airlines that charge for every little thing. It's crazy to pay for a carry-on or a paper boarding pass."

"They charge for a boarding pass! What else do they charge for besides the ticket?" The second flight attendant asks as they criticized the airline I was speaking of. Little do they know that the attacks on September 11 changed the aviation industry.

"They charge low fares, but then you have to pay for the physical boarding pass, baggage, beverages, which seat you want and more."

"Well, welcome to Americonic. If you need anything, please feel free to let one of us know," she says, and they both return their attention to preparing dinner service.

I smile and turn around, heading back up front. I glance at my watch and see that it's 18:50. Dad should be stepping out any second if my memory serves me right. But I worry about the delay with Marge creating a domino effect. I scoot around the beverage cart again and pass by the siblings still playing the same round. My heart just sinks when I pass them. Moving forward, I stand by the booth, waiting for Dad to step out of the cockpit.

The door opens, and there's my father. He steps away from the cockpit, and I study him, analyzing his movements, his gestures, his handsome face, his proud, pressed uniform.

He walks casually past me and the two lavatories, stepping into the galley. His cologne follows his body, and its fragrance leaves behind a warm spice and woody note.

The flight attendant who took their coffee orders realizes what he's there for. "Captain, I'm so sorry. Here's your coffee. I got sidetracked with helping Marge prepare the ovens for dinner service."

Marge points to the oven, slapping it. "Brand new aircraft, and this industry-leading oven Americonic bought won't turn on." I watch from the booth as Dad inspects the oven, trying to diagnose it.

After a few moments of fidgeting with the machine, he grabs the interphone on the wall behind Marge. "Dan, it's Paul. Do me a favor, would you. Have Ray reset the breaker for the forward galley." The light bulb over the counter flickers as the power is reset.

Dad returns the phone to the port on the wall and tries the on and off switch for the oven. A red light illuminates and the flight attendants are thrilled. "Thank you, Captain." Marge turns the dial to max, and the ovens are filled with tinfoil covered dinner trays.

"Why can't all Captains be as resourceful as you are?" Judy says.

"Those old scrooges are about to retire once we get the jumbo 747 in regular service. I'll be moving up to fly that queen," Dad says proudly before picking up the tray containing the coffee cups.

Then he turns to me and smiles. *Oh no! He must have sensed that I was staring at him.*

Still smiling, he puts down the tray and heads my way. The butterflies in my stomach take flight. *How am I supposed to not tell him that he'll be dead in a few minutes? I just don't understand.*

I can't take it anymore. I start to have a panic attack. Deciding to go back to my real life, I race into the lavatory, securing the door behind me. I stare into the mirror, afraid to touch it.

I hear a knocking sound on the door and Dad's voice. "Ma'am, are you okay? I didn't mean to frighten you."

"Keep it together, Jackie," I say out loud. Not responding to Dad, I reach up and touch the mirror, closing my eyes as I do. I wait for a few moments, and nothing happens.

"What the —" I say, frantically pawing at the mirror. "Why isn't it working?" Now, I really *do* start to panic. Every second I spend touching the mirror brings us one second closer to disaster.

CHAPTER 9

Three chimes sound through the speakers overhead. I look up, curious, at Marge and Judy who have unbelted themselves and risen from their jumpseats. Marge returns the interphone to its port, and Judy joins her in walking to the forward galley.

Three more flight attendants, from the rear cabin, rush into the first-class galley, closing the curtain behind them. The passengers around me are confused and scared. The sounds of terror ricochet through the cabin. For the first time, I can hear fear.

I focus strictly on trying to listen to their conversation, but I can't hear anything they're saying clearly. A minute later, the curtain is pulled back, and they all exit. No smiles, no frowns, just sealed lips with a stern face and heads held high. They've fallen back on their training, and there is no time to focus on their emotion.

As the other flight attendants jump into action in the cabin, Judy stays behind in the galley and starts opening cabinets with purpose. She is focused and quiet and knows exactly which cabinets hold the supplies she's looking for. She swiftly and calmly pulls out multiple containers labeled first aid. She also places a bunch of small brandy bottles on the countertop. I watch her, as I have nothing but time. Which is ironic, considering the reason I'm here.

Judy then turns her attention to the coffee pots. She presses the blue illuminated *brew* button. Usually when she presses this button, it is to make a warm drink for her passengers or even herself. However, now she presses this button with the intent to sterilize hand towels. She is getting supplies and preparing to take care of the injured.

She is executing her job with ease. Her training has given her the necessary skills to get herself, her passengers and her crew through the worst day of their lives. She shows no emotion as the hot water brews, only determination. Every few seconds, she replaces the pot and brews more hot water, then places the hand towels into the pot she exchanged from the machine.

Soon, she has multiple towels ready to apply pressure to open wounds and the brandy available to sterilize wounds. What smart, quick thinking on her part. Flight attendants are nothing if not resourceful, and Judy proves it.

The remaining flight attendants pass through the cabin assessing passengers, seat by seat. I keep hearing the call bell sound, but not in any sequential order. Random alarms keep ringing. I go against my better judgement and loosen my belt just enough that I am able to twist my body and look back.

The cabin interior is gruesome. Ceiling panels are missing or lying on the floor, the aisle is littered with blankets, papers, personal effects and other unsecured items. The force of the blast created this huge mess. The three other flight attendants are about a third of the way down the cabin, and a handful of flight attendant call lights are illuminated via a small yellow light bulb in the overhead passenger service unit.

Marge is standing inside the galley. I lean forward trying to see what she is doing. Not until Judy leaves do I see that she has a green checklist in her hand. She must be reviewing their company procedures for an emergency landing.

Another flight attendant, whom I had met earlier in passing with the beverage cart, storms up. Her hair is a frizzy mess. "We need bandages and clean cloths." Judy understands, filling a serving tray with burning moist towels from the coffee pot and placing boxes of bandages on the tray too. Once filled, she leaves the galley, and Judy throws in new towels and returns the coffee pot to brew more hot water.

A different flight attendant comes up to the galley and requests the same items. Judy again loads a tray, and she departs. The coordination between these women is very organized and well performed.

After a good ten minutes, a single bell is heard. Marge picks up the phone. "This is Marge. Great, thank you." She hangs up and places the green checklist in front of her on the counter. Marge and another flight attendant, who had come to the front, start at the front of the cabin and walk their way back. Marge stays on floor level while the other attendant, rather short without her heels on, grabs items from the overhead storage shelving, tossing them down to the passengers below.

Marge walks in front of her, her voice elevated. "Take off your shoes, eyeglasses, and neckties, and place them in the seat back pockets in front of you. When we give the command to brace, wrap your arms under your knees and keep your heads down until we come to a complete stop. At that time, we will give the order to evacuate. Raise your seat backs to the upright and locked position. Check the security of your seat belts. Tighten them as much as you can, please. They should be uncomfortably tight."

Next to me, there's a couple praying together and holding hands. "Lord, please get us through this," I hear them say. *Amen,* I think to myself.

After their walk-through is complete and Marge has returned to the forward galley, another bell sounds, and Marge answers the phone. Immediately, she announces across the cabin "Line one." The she returns to the phone and begins a brief conversation via the interphone. *Line one is a code for them to all be on the phone for a briefing.* It wasn't too hard for me to put that together in my head.

I watch as the color drains from her face. Turning toward the galley where Judy is listening in, her face tells a different story: fear. Looking back at Marge, I see her take a moment to collect herself, then she presses the button on the phone again to provide instructions. Only this one isn't for the faint of heart.

"Ladies and gentlemen, the captain has informed the crew that we may have make an ocean landing. Our estimated time of impact is eight minutes. Please reach under your seat and locate your life vest. Remove the life vest from the pouch and slip it over your head, securing the strap around your waist. There is a light that will activate when it touches the water. *Please* do not inflate the vest until you are outside the aircraft. We will be coming around the cabin to assist with any questions you have. Please remain calm."

Once she finishes, I reach below my seat cushion and open the flap. Pulling the pouch from its slot. I tear off the protective seal and remove the yellow life vest, unfolding it. I place it over my head and then lean forward to secure the strap around my waist, careful not to inflate it.

The passengers around me do the same. Many of them are groaning, and some of them are moaning with fear. I have a brief thought about the two children I saw playing checkers earlier.

Without a moment to think, I reach up and press the call button. The light pops on and soon Marge arrives. "How can I help you?"

"No, I am fine. What about the two kids in row 10? Are they okay?" I shriek.

"Yes ma'am. They are safe," she says. "Is there anything else?"

Realizing the fear that those two must be in, I whimpered. "Are they traveling alone?"

"Yes. They are unaccompanied minors," she says. I unbuckle my seat belt immediately. "And just where do you think you are going?"

"Those poor babies are away from their family on one of the worst experiences they will ever face in their lives." I hissed. "I am going to sit with them and comfort them both until this ordeal is over and they are safe on the ground." I was expecting a full on argument with Marge, but to my surprise, she agreed.

Grabbing me by the hand, she escorted me to row ten—the first row in tourist class. "George? Cindy? This is my good friend —"

She pauses for me to answer. "Jackie."

"Jackie, and she is going to sit with you and help you prepare for landing, okay?' Marge says and advises the children to allow me to sit in between them. I sit and fasten my belt. Before I talk to the kids, I double check to make sure that their belts are secured around their waists and the life vests are fitted properly.

"Jackie?" Cindy says with tears in her eyes. I make eye contact with her. "Are we going to make it?"

Not sure of the answer myself, I grab her hand and George's. "We are going to be just fine. My dad is the pilot, and I know that he will do everything he can." My reassurance provides a few moments of relaxation to the children.

Our diversion to peace snaps when there's a burst of air, then another and another. I look around frantic trying to understand where the sound is coming from. I see that three passengers ahead of us have already pulled the red strings on their life vests and the sound of air was them inflating.

Marge looks electric with rage. She realizes what has happened and proceeds to the forward galley. She then comes out of the galley, moment later, with a steak knife and a few extra life vests. She stomps to the younger woman in first class who had inflated the vests, and at first, I'm afraid she's going to attack her. Using her steak knife, she pops the inflated vest and it loses it pressure. "Put on these ones," she orders, handing her the new life vests. "And *don't* inflate them until you are outside of this aircraft." The scared woman agrees nodding her head.

Marge then continues on her march. Stomping past me and the children, she pops three more life vests and gives the same order to them about waiting to inflate.

"Why is she doing that? Aren't the floaties supposed to blow up?" George whimpers.

"Yes, but we have to wait until we exit the airplane to inflate."

Once Marge had distributed the extra vests throughout the cabin, she returns to the front entry and picks up the microphone again. "DO NOT INFLATE YOUR LIFE VEST UNTIL YOU ARE OUTSIDE OF THE AIRCRAFT!" she commands. *That little flight attendant sure can stop traffic with her mighty voice.*

After a few minutes, a pilot exits the cockpit, but it's not Dad. It's one of the other men. He starts surveying the cabin, feeling around the doors, broken side panels, and eventually the ceiling where the green aluminum is exposed. *He must be checking for structural damage.* When he approaches my row, I reach out and grab him by the arm. "Is Paul okay?" I hiss.

"He's fine and at the controls," he assures and continues his quest in the cabin.

The plane makes a gradual left turn, nothing like our earlier dive. I assume we're headed for the airport, and I trust that Dad will get us there. After a minute, I hear the two chimes again.

A shaky male voice comes over the public address system. "Folks, we are making our descent into Halifax. I need you to listen very carefully. We will be landing *fast and hard.* You must remain *seated and belts fastened* until we come to a complete stop. *Please.* Follow the flight attendants' commands, and I promise that we will get through this together."

At the completion of his announcement, Marge meets the other pilot at the divider between the first-class and tourist-class cabins. From my seat with the children, I can hear what they are saying as this pilot was kind of loud.

"Marge, I need you to move people away from the blast area and put them in empty seats anywhere else. Everyone must have a belt to strap into when we touch down."

"Dan, what are the chances that the aircraft will keep its structural integrity?" Marge whispers discreetly in his ear.

Dan gathers his thoughts. "Based on my survey, I believe that the aircraft will survive the landing. We lost engine three shortly after the blast."

"Will that hurt with trying to stop us on the runway?

"No, we have three other engines that are running smoothly. My only concern is the runway length. It's a bit short, but we don't have a choice," Dan states.

Marge shrugged. "Okay, thank you, Dan. Is there anything else that I can do before you head back up?"

"No, Marge," he says and proceeds to the cockpit.

Marge walks out of my sight, but I hear her voice on the loudspeaker. "Line one."

Moments later, the other flight attendants join in the forward galley for one last briefing. When they emerge, the crew, who is stationed in the rear section, walk back and scan each passenger. They pass us and do not make any remarks.

Judy stops by our row and checks in on the two minors. She confirmed that their belts are still secured — even though I double-checked them earlier.

A high-low chime sounds again about a minute later. "Ladies and gentlemen, as we make our final approach, we are going to dim the lights in the cabin for your eyes to adjust. Please use the pillows, blankets and coats we passed out as cushioning for the landing."

The cabin lights flicker and turn off. My eyes go black as I wait for them to adjust to the environment. I have my hands holding the children's hand and praying. *Lord, please keep us safe.*

When my eyes adjust, I can see the lights of land through the open windows. Lights mean that there is a sign of hope. Maybe just the sign we need.

CHAPTER 10

I have no way of knowing if I'm about to die. I think about Candice, hoping that she's safe with Melinda's team in Washington. I don't know if I'll ever see her again.

My thoughts are interrupted by a loud male voice over the public address system. "BRACE FOR LANDING!"

I try to catch a glimpse of what's happening out the window on my right. The shade is still open. I can see city lights in the darkness. I feel a faint flicker of hope as we get closer and closer to the runway. *Closer to safety.*

From their positions on the jump seat, the flight attendants shout.

"Brace, brace, brace! Heads down, stay down!"

"Brace, brace, brace! Heads down, stay down!"

"Brace, brace, brace! Heads down, stay down!"

Together, the children and I bend forward. I let go of their hands and instruct them to hold their own hands under their legs as tight as possible. Keeping our hands locked together, we sit in an eerie state all the while commands are being shouted.

The plane's eight wheels smack the ground simultaneously. The roar of the engine goes wild as the reversers are engaged. I can hear the tires screaming below us as the brakes are applied. I'm thrown forward, my seatbelt digging painfully into my waist. I sneak a peek at the children, who are crying but still in the brace positions.

Loud screeching fills the cabin as the brakes lock the wheels and the aircraft starts to skid. I can smell burning rubber, and I wonder how long the tires will hold out.

My eyes are closed so tight that I'm unsure if I'll ever be able to open them again. I don't want to see death if it should arrive. The airplane shakes and roars down the runway. The other passengers have grown quiet, or I simply can't hear them over the roar.

We have been traveling down the runway for at least 10-15 seconds since we touched down. The airplane is not stopping, and having never been to this airport, I hope there is no cliff at the end of the runway.

Suddenly, the children and I are jolted to the right. George smacks his head against the wall panel. The aircraft has pivoted to the left in a violent fashion. The sounds of metal ripping apart fill the cabin.

The plane stops. The smell of jet fuel fills the cabin. There is nothing to do but wait.

I open my eyes and take a look around. The cabin is silent, except for quiet prayers among the passengers. The fear has set in, and the screams, groans, and shrieks are mute.

I stare at the two attendants at the front. *Once they move, I'll move.* The stench of burning rubber still permeates the cabin.

The silence is broken when a male voice yells through the overhead speakers, "EVACUATE!"

The two attendants jump up and go to their stations. The lights in the cabin illuminate, revealing that the structure itself is still in one piece. With a quick and violent tug, I see Marge throw open the heavy door and hear a loud whooshing sound. *The emergency slides.*

"Come this way!" call the flight attendants. "Calmly and safely. Leave *everything*." We hear them, but no one is moving. People are frozen in their seats.

Snapping back into reality when the smell of smoke hits my nostrils, I unbuckle my belt, forcing myself to get to my feet. I bend over and unbuckle Cindy's belt first, then George's. I point to the front and tell the two kids to head forward and get out. They follow my command and I watch as Marge sends them down the now inflated slide to safety. I turn around to help other passengers get out. One by one, other passengers head towards the front and the passengers in the rear head for the other exits that have been opened.

The cabin is filling with thick and dark black smoke, and I'm sure a fire has started. *I hope it doesn't spread to the fuel tanks.* If the fire trucks can make it here in time, we may be able to save the plane and figure out what happened.

My fear is brought to life when I see flames through the windows on the right side. The orange glow provides me with a new level of fear. *I survived the explosion and the landing, but now I have to survive the fire.*

One by one, I guide distressed people to the front, and before I know it, windows begin to burst from the elevated temperatures near the flames. The lights in the cabin flicker as the light bulbs burn out. The interior is hot.

Standing near the middle of the cabin, I see the floor in the aisle begin to glow. *The fire is coming through the floor.*

"EVERYONE OUT! NOW!" I turn around and see my dad bellowing at the few remaining people on board. I turn to join him, but my heel sinks into the floor. *Oh, God. The floor is melting beneath me with the heat from the fire.* It dawns on me that I am standing near or over the center fuel tank.

"DAD! I'M STUCK. HELP ME!" I have never been so frightened. *I survived time travel, I survived the crash, and now I'm just going to… burn to death?*

Dad races over to help me. He tries to get my foot out of the heel, but these shoes are snug and meant to stay on.

Finally, Dad gives an almighty yank and pulls me free. Just as we stand, fire surrounds us, engulfing the cabin and blocks the forward and rear exits. *We're trapped.*

I turn to my father. "What do we do now?" Wordlessly, he gathers me in a hug. *This is the first time I've hugged this man in fifty year's and it will be the last.* He holds me so tight I have trouble breathing.

Then he speaks directly into my ear. "JACKIE! What date did you leave in 2023?" I look at him in confusion. "Jackie, tell me!"

Forcing myself to focus, I reply, "July 7!"

I watch as dad closes his eyes tightly and holds me even tighter. His eyes open and turn a brilliant white color. *Why are his eyes a different color?*

The smell of smoke disappears, and we're surrounded by blackness. Dad is still holding me, but I feel something scratching at my arm. My eyes open and I see a sea of different colored lights shining through a dark field.

My ears are penetrated by a loud noise coming from my right. I look over and see four large yellow spotlights growing bigger and bigger. As they come closer, I see a red flashing light. The noise only gets louder, and then I recognize it.

The mighty 747 races by at top speed before climbing into the evening sky. The large yellow lights were on the aircraft. As the plane fades away, I stand up and see concrete in the mixed of the little lights. Twisting my body around and around, I stop when I see a building with more planes. *We're at an airport.*

Suddenly, a vehicle approaches with red and blue lights flashing. Those lights should trigger a fear complex, but I am so relieved to see help coming. When the car stops, the officer flips on the bright spotlight illuminating the field around me.

I look around the area — now that it's lit — and see Dad lying in the grass. *Thank God it's not winter.* He is unconscious when I get to him. I drop to my knees and rock his shoulders, trying to wake him.

His eyes open and stare at me, but not in the white color as before. Just plain and simple eyes. "Dad!" I roar. "Are you okay? Are you hurt?" I survey his body looking for wounds.

"I'm fine, honey," he says, sitting up and smacking his hands together to wipe away any dust.

Before I can ask another question, we hear a shout from the car. The officer demands we stand up and walk toward him slowly. Both dad and I are handcuffed and placed into the car's rear holding compartment like criminals.

"What are you two doing out here?" the officer demands. "This is a restricted area. You could have gotten yourselves killed by one of these giant airplanes," he continues as he drives us toward the terminal. If he only knew the dangers we endured earlier.

The officer drove us to the police station in the airport and booked us into jail. Dad and I were separated into different areas. When I received my one phone call, I called the only number I knew. Candice's cell.

The phone rings for a few moments. "Hello?" Candice says.

"Candice!" I cheered. "It's Jackie. Dad and I are —"

She cuts me off. "At the Halifax airport police station?"

"I don't understand. How did you know?" I ask.

She hangs up the phone after saying that she would explain in about five minutes. Sure enough, she enters the holding area with Melinda and Agent Taylor. Candice runs over to me. We embrace each other and hug securely. Once we break apart, Melinda gives me a hug, and so does Agent Taylor.

"I don't understand," I squeak. "How did you know that I would be here?"

Melinda jumps in. "Well, when the aircraft burned to the ground and the only two people who were missing were the captain and an unmanifested woman in a red dress, my boss knew what happened. Or, at least he knew what happened to Paul."

Agent Taylor interjected. "And, there were no dental remains to identify. Adding to the case that the fire was so hot, it burned bone."

A look of confusion and possible exhaustion still held my face. Melinda continued. "Ken set up a special operation for this date and this time. His plan was to meet your father at the last known site of the aircraft. Given that your dad would always end up in the future at the last known location, it was a solid plan."

"If it was the plan, then why were we arrested?" I shriek.

"The cops would have locked us in the loony bin if we would have told them about our plan. The mayor is a longtime friend, and when I told him that I need two personnel released from custody, he called the station himself and spoke to the police chief."

Amazed with how resourceful Melinda is, my mind tracks back to Dad. "Where is Dad?"

"He is in another cell. I figured that you and Candice would like to see him together." She says, and we exit the holding cell, proceeding down the hallway. The guard unlocks the door, and we burst in. Both Candice and I run up to Dad, knocking him to the floor.

"Candice?" he says.

"Hi, Dad!" she shouts and holds him tight. "It's great to see you, finally."

Melinda speaks over our emotions. "Mr. Jette, welcome to 2023!" Dad just smiles. I think he's a little stunned. "Shall we go?" she asks and points towards the door.

"Where?" I ask.

"We are headed for Bluefin Cove on a charter Air Force plane."

Dad asks, "What the hell is Bluefin Cove?"

"I'll tell you on the way, Dad," I tell him. "We've got a lot to catch up on."

CHAPTER 11

For the whole plane ride, Dad stares at me and Candice from his seat. I find it difficult to believe that this thirty-something-year-old man is my father. The last hour of our lives has been magical and terrifying. *Yes, I have my dad back, and I didn't die in the airplane, but… I disturbed the past.*

"I know you're all tired," Melinda says, "but I made reservations at the Bluefin Hotel for Agent Taylor and myself. This way, you three can sleep in your own beds tonight. The flight should be about an hour or so."

Ah… heading back home. As much as I love the big city, I've truly missed our little town of Bluefin Cove.

While taxiing down the runway, I look over at my dad. He's gazing out at the runway lights. I get the feeling something's bothering him, and I bet I can guess what it is. *He's 52 years in the future… and I bet he misses Mom.* What a terrible roll of the dice. *He lost his wife, but he gets to keep his daughters… only now we're both older than he is.*

Once we get up to cruising altitude, I unfasten my seatbelt and get up from my chair. "Dad?"

He turns his head, and I see tears rolling down his cheeks. *This is a man who just landed a stricken jetliner and jumped into a fire to save me. Now he's crying uncontrollably.*

He wipes away his tears. "Yes, Jackie?" I crouch down so I'm eye level with him.

"Do you want to ask anything?" I say. "I mean, I know you must have a ton of questions."

"Where's Bluefin Cove?" he asks, which makes me smile. Everything we've been through, and he wants to know where we live. *I guess it's a start.*

"Dad, Bluefin Cove is where Candice and I live, up in Maine. After your plane went missing in 1971, we moved there with the settlement money from the government."

Candice jumps in. "Well, since Dad was able to land the aircraft, all of the passengers and crew were able to evacuate."

I tilt my head, curious. "What else changed?"

"Well, Dad was presumed killed when the airplane went up in flames. As for you, you were classified as a stowaway, and no one at Americonic knows how you snuck on board."

Melinda interjects, "Jackie, thank you for going against my wishes and saving your dad. I have an idea, and I want to hear your thoughts on it."

I nod, waiting for her to go on.

"I want your dad to become your handler for any future assignments. His experience can help you a lot."

I meet my dad's eyes with a grin. "Well, what do you think? Dad, would you want to semi-retire?"

"Well," Dad considers. "What's the year now? 2023? That makes me just about 88 years old, so I guess I'm due for a lighter schedule," he chuckles. "Why not?"

"Great," Melinda says. "I want to give you a month off before we talk about any assignments. This way, you and Candice can get to know your dad."

"Sounds good," I confirm. Then I notice Candice's fabulous pearl necklace. "Candice, where did the pearls come from?"

She stretches her neck to show them off, then lifts her hair so I can see the matching earrings. "These are my birth mother's pearls that survived the crash in 1954. Melinda's boss, Kenneth Gable kept them in a safe space for me. I decided I'll wear them for good luck now, since they brought you both home."

Dad whips around and stares at the necklace. "Christine Carter! I told her the airplane was going to crash while we were in the air. She begged me to take you back with me."

"Why did you tell her?" Melinda asks. "All of Mr. Jenkins' reports indicate that you never told anyone about your gift or your assignments. So, why her?"

"That was an unusual flight. When I time-traveled, I ended up in the seat next to her and Candice. Charles was in front of us. When I suddenly appeared, Christine was stunned to see a stranger materialize in the seat next to her, so I had to say *something.* "

"Why didn't you try to save the aircraft?" I ask. *I know I could never just let all those people die.*

"Jackie, that crash changed history for millions of people in the decades to come. The Comet was a great airplane with a fatal flaw. By the time I arrived inside the plane, the cracks had already formed in the outer skin." I can see he's tearing up again. None of this is easy.

Agent Taylor finally breaks his silence from the back of the cabin to say, "That's right! All those terrible accidents provided Boeing engineers with the necessary information to design a pressurized cabin."

"Paul's right," Melinda confirms. "The crash had to happen for the greater good. People had to die, but those deaths were not in vain."

I do remember seeing a history documentary about the Boeing 707, and there was a part about the test of a new fuselage based off the facts of metal fatigue from the Comet crashes.

I then look at my dad, who is the Boeing 707 captain with all of this experience, and ask him, "Dad, did you know that the wing design for the 707 was created based on an idea by a German engineer during World War II?"

He looks at me and gives me the best response a dad could. "You know that I am a captain on the 707, right?" We all laugh, and I give him a hug. I had to grow up without a dad, and now I have him back.

The remainder of the flight is uneventful until we touch down at the airfield in Maine. I look out the window to see a sea of runway and taxi lights with hangars and lots of airport vehicles moving around.

"Agent Taylor?" I ask. "What field are we at? I thought we were going to the same one we left two days ago? This is a full-scale airport operation. This airport has lights, and the one we departed was nearly abandoned in a grassy field."

"This is the same field. But… it's a bit different. When you and Paul didn't step off the burning aircraft in 1971, Melinda's former boss advised the military that we need this base to be operational, even if it's only a training facility."

"But, why?" I persist. "Ken had no idea that we would be coming to Bluefin Cove."

"Let's just say that Ken did not make that decision until a year or so after you all moved here. He trusted his gut and his gut was correct," Melinda concludes.

Agent Taylor turns to Melinda. "Do you want to tell them? After all, it's your project now."

"This isn't just a training facility," Melinda tells us.

"What is it, then?" I ask.

The airplane comes to a stop and the engines become quiet.

"Why don't we all go and see for ourselves?" Melinda says. She leads us down the aircraft stairs, and we're greeted by a black SUV similar to the one that Agent Taylor drove. I spin in circles looking around at the numerous buildings and coast guard aircraft parked around us. We pile in and head for the nearest hangar.

"Where are we going?" I ask.

The car comes to a stop in front of the hangar after a short drive. I can see letters at the top of the building, but I can't make them out in the dark.

Melinda makes a call on her cell phone and says, "We're here, Sally. Please turn on the lights." Melinda disconnects and puts the phone back into her pocket. Candice, Dad and I look around, waiting for something to happen.

After a few moments, five light bulbs snap on at the top of the building. They take a moment to warm up, changing from a dark blue glow to a brighter white. Once they're bright enough, I read the sign. JETTE INDUSTRIES is emblazoned on the hangar in bold print.

"What's *that*?" Dad asks.

"Jette Industries is the name of your company," Melinda explains. "It's the largest aircraft leasing company on the East Coast."

"Aircraft leasing? We lease aircraft now?" I whisper to Candice. "What's going on here?"

Smiling, Melinda takes me by the hand. Together, we enter the massive hangar, stepping into a grand and imposing lobby. One wall is covered with photos of aircraft from all around the world. There's a huge poster of Dad standing in front of an Americonic aircraft, covering a large section of the wall. Dad comes in behind me and studies the blown-up photo of himself.

"That was just a week ago," he says, "on the same aircraft that burned in Halifax."

"Can you explain?" I plead with Melinda. "None of this makes any sense to me."

"When you were both presumed dead in the fire, Ken left instructions for his successor to make sure a building was ready in 2023. Given that the Coast Guard was looking for a new facility, I was able to have leeway with the buildings. He knew that something was going to happen and wanted to make sure everything was ready. Last year, this building was finished, and I had all of our material, supplies and files moved here."

"Why?" I ask.

Melinda leads us down a long corridor to a security door. She swipes her badge and enters a code. The door swings open to reveal another hallway, this one lined with offices. The first door we pass has the name *Stephanie Wilson* on the name plate.

"Whose office is that? Not Stephanie the *designer*?" I ask.

"Yes, it is!" Melinda affirms as we continue on. "I had her transferred to our new office here. I just love her work and I want to make sure that she has all the tools she needs."

The next office is on the left, and it has Agent Taylor's name on it. "I live near here too," Agent Taylor says, smacking the door affectionately. "I get to work on assignments and drive you guys around when you need a lift."

Melinda keeps walking, then points to a third door, with my father's name on it. "Mr. Jette, this is your new office. I had all of Mr. Jenkins' files and notes brought here," she says.

Dad looks confused. "Why isn't it *his* office, then?"

"Mr. Jenkins is retired now. He only stayed on part-time to be Jackie's boss at the law firm."

The office next to Dad's turns out to be for me. The name plate says *Jackie Jette*. "I'll get you your keys when you come back to work in a month," Melinda says.

Finally, we arrive at a door at the end of the hall. Melinda swipes her badge again and enters a code. The door swings open and we all enter her office.

This one is more of a suite, with a briefing room on one side, and a vault room on the left, similar to the one we saw in Washington. My father whistles through his teeth. "I can't believe this evidence is still in such good shape after so many years."

"Mr. Jenkins took good care of it, Mr. Jette." Melinda says. "Well," "she smiles, "that completes the tour. What do you think?"

"Candice, did you know about all this?" I ask her.

"Nope. I had no idea until we landed here. I knew the airport was still here, but I never paid attention to the hangars. Plus, we never come out this way."

"Dad, when we left for Washington, this airfield was just grass, with a pavement runway," I tell him.

He chuckles. "Jackie, whenever you go back and change the past, things are going to be different. It's perfectly normal. Or — as normal as you can expect, with time travel."

We chat for a few minutes more, but then the day's events take their toll and I start yawning. A hot shower and my own cozy bed start sounding awfully nice.

"Agent Taylor, would you please drive us home to Bluefin Cove?" I ask, as we return to the lobby at the front of the building.

"I sure can!" he responds, heading out to bring his car around.

"Melinda," I say, "thank you for everything. If I wasn't so tired, I'd love to know more. But I'm just so exhausted."

Melinda gives me a hug. "I understand, and Agent Taylor will get you home. I'll give you some space for a month to let you spend family time together."

"But don't you want to know what happened on the aircraft?" I solicited.

Melinda giggles. "Jackie, it's been fifty-one years. The investigation can wait a few more weeks."

She walks us out to Agent Taylor's car, which turns out to be electric. "New car?" I asked through the open window.

"He has to have a more fuel-efficient car," Melinda explains. "After all, he's a big executive with Jette Industries. He has to look the part. Plus, the government loves energy-saving devices."

Dad gets in the passenger side, while Candice and I sit in back. Dad examines the dashboard, which must look space age to his eyes. Then he looks up through the car ceiling.

"Whoa!" he says in amazement. "I can see the stars." Then, "Why is the motor so quiet? Is this one of those foreign cars?"

"Dad," I explain, "this is a Tesla. It's all electric and has no gas-powered components." I point out the battery percentage on the dash.

Dad turns to Agent Taylor. "When the battery gets low, does it charge like a golf cart?" His question, so adorable.

"Mr. Jette, when I get home every night, I have a cable in the trunk that plugs into an outlet in my garage. It charges overnight, and in the morning, I have three hundred miles of range."

"What happens if you get low and you're not home?" Dad asks. I always watched the TV shows with goofy dads, and now I have one too. It's so awesome.

"Dad, a lot of businesses have charging stations. It's like a gas pump, but you use a credit card or your smartwatch to pay, and then the pump charges the car's battery."

"Smartwatch?" Dad persists. "Is that some sort of check?" Candice and I look at each other, but we're both too tired to explain.

"Yep!" Candice chirps. "That's exactly what it is."

By then, Agent Taylor's pulling into the driveway of our home. I've never been so thrilled to be back.

"Thanks for the ride," I say, getting out of the car. "Get home safe."

But Agent Taylor just chuckles. "Luckily, I don't have a far drive. I bought the blue house down at the end of the street."

"The old Miller places! No one's lived there in years." *The neighborhood kids used to tell each other ghost stories about that house.*

"I have it pretty fixed up. When you ride down to the café, you'll have to check it out." With that, Agent Taylor backs down the driveway and speeds off down the street.

Candice and I lead Dad to the front porch, and he follows us inside. I close the door once he enters and lock it. The house comfortingly familiar, for which I'm grateful.

"Dad, can we give you a tour tomorrow when you wake up?" We're all just about falling down from sheer exhaustion. Candice shows Dad to the spare room under the staircase.

I head up the stairs to my room and close the door. I look longingly at my bed. Tonight, that bed is my reward for a job well done.

First things first! A shower to wash off the smoke and saltwater. As the bathroom starts to fill up with steam, I unzip my red dress and let it fall to the floor.

The water runs over my body, and I let it wash away the stress of the day. I catch myself nodding off with a headful of shampoo and decide that it's time to hit the hay. I slip on a faded old Bluefin Bowling League T shirt and slip between my silky sheets. I have no idea what time it is, but my eyes close and I'm instantly asleep.

CHAPTER 12

The smell of sizzling bacon fills my nostrils. I toss and turn, trying my best to stay asleep… but the temptation of breakfast is too much.

Yanking the bedclothes off and sitting up, I feel like I was hit by a bus and then dragged a mile. The last time I felt this way was the morning after my fiftieth birthday party, nearly three years ago.

The water is cold when it splashes my face, but it does the trick. I rinse my eyes, trying to remove the crust built up during the night. Then I peer at myself in the mirror. My hair is a twisted mess, and there are dark circles under my eyes. While I tug and pull at my hair, I hear a knock at the door, then it opens. "Candice, is that you?"

"Yes! And your breakfast is getting cold!"

Picking out a simple shirt and pants from my closet, I change and make my way down the stairs, hoping to see Dad at the table.

"It's about time you got down here," Candice grumbles. "Here's your breakfast."

"You made all this yourself?"

"Pfff, of course! I used to cook for James all the time, didn't I?"

Candice loved to cook for her husband, James. He would be on the road three to five days at a time, and she would cook a bunch of different meals and portion them into containers that he could reheat on the road.

I look around the sparkling clean kitchen. "How did you make all this food and clean up so fast?"

Candice lets out a guilty laugh. "Okay, fine. I didn't cook anything. I woke up early and went down to the café. Ruby's cooks are so much better at making breakfast than I am."

I rise from my chair and walk around the table to give her a hug. "Thank you for getting me breakfast, sis." I tell her. "I knew it was Ruby's from the first bite. I just wanted to tease you."

"You're *so* mean."

"You know you missed me."

Candice is eager for me to finish eating, since she wants to show Dad around town and buy him some clothes. This morning he had to borrow Candice's bathrobe, since his clothes from last night were in tatters.

"Where's Dad?" I ask.

"Out on the porch. I gave him a left-over fundraiser shirt from last year's gala and a pair of sweatpants I found in the back of my closet."

I grab my coffee and head for the door. He's rocking in one of the chairs, staring out the ocean. When he sees me, he rises from the chair to give me a hug.

"How did you sleep" I ask, taking a seat next to his.

"I slept okay. It's not the bed I'm used to."

"Dad, the bed you're used to is long gone."

Dad looks around. "Where is your mother? Does she have her own place here in Bluefin Cove?"

Candice exits through the front door and joins our conversation. "She died, Dad," she says. "A couple of years ago now. But she never stopped loving you. She never remarried."

A shadow passes across my dad's face, and I search for ways to comfort him.

"She was a strong woman, Dad. She never let anything stop her. When we moved here from New York, she devoted herself to bringing the town into the twenty-first century."

"That's right," Candice says. "She was the one who did all the fundraisers and bake sales to build the Bluefin Bowling Center."

"She was a top bowler for years," I remark. "Mom also helped add new books to the library and create after-school programs for the local kids."

"She really did all of that?" Dad asks. "As a… as a widow?"

"Dad, we were very young children. When we grew up, she made sure to keep things positive." Candice says.

We spend the next two hours talking about mom's charity events and her retirement years, though her retirement was really just a second career. These rocking chairs haven't heard so much gossip since Mom died.

I feel around my pocket for my phone, but I must have left it charging on my nightstand.

"I am going to run up and grab my phone," I tell Candice and Dad. "Candice, should we take Dad into town?"

"Absolutely! You need to see my shop, Dad," Candice beams.

"Do you have a Sears or something near here where I can get some clothes in my size?" Dad asks, tugging at his sweatpants.

"Sure, Dad," I tell him. "Not a Sears, but we have a local shop here in town. Rita will take good care of you."

I drop of my coffee cup in the kitchen sink and race up the stairs to add a touch of make-up and throw on a pair of sneakers. I'm finished with heels for the time being — I don't care how comfortable they are.

We pile into the old Buick, with Dad sitting behind the wheel. Candice stares at him for a moment and then hands him the keys. Amazed by the 1990s Buick, he drives it well for not having a current license. Dad looks at me in the rearview mirror.

"Where's your driver's license?" he asks.

"Well, I never learned how to drive. I have my bike."

"Why not?"

"Bluefin's so small, and I was never good at it when Mom took me out for lessons. There's a scratch on the bumper that's my fault, plus a telephone pole in town I tangled with."

Dad laughs. "I bet Mom never told you that when we first got together, she hit a grocery shopping cart two days after we bought the car."

We all burst out laughing. It's so weird to have someone tell us stories from the distant past. *Having Dad back is great... but strange.*

Candice stops in front of her shop. We get out of the car, and for the first time, Candice gets to show her dad all about her world.

CHAPTER 13

Closing the heavy Buick door behind me, I follow Candice and Dad into the shop. This place used to be owned by an older couple who retired to Florida a few years back, and Candice bought it, looking for a new start after James's death.

She spent the first month in her new store painting, building new displays and adding shelving to make room for greeting cards. I'm so proud of all of her hard work — the place looks like a million bucks.

Next door to Candice's shop is a bakery, which accounts for the fresh cinnamon smell that tends to waft inside. And on the other side of her store, there's the Bluefin Coffee Company. Our dear friend, Ryker Miller, opened the store about fifteen years ago. We went to high school together, and he was always the one with a cup of coffee, even at the age of sixteen. No one was surprised when he built his own coffee shop in town.

Across the street are a few more town landmarks. The first and probably the most important is Grandview Clothing Company, and next to that is Frank's Hardware and our local physician, Dr. Haven Pillars.

I stand back to examine Candice's window display. The annual Bowling League Banquet is right around the corner, and she and Grace must have worked overtime on this massive, three-tiered arrangement.

The first tier has bowling pins mixed in with floral arrangements, and there are even a few pairs of shoes. *Love it!* The second tier has roses, daisies, sunflowers, and lilies, all spouting out of actual retired bowling balls gaining a new life as vases.

Right in the middle, there's a big, hand-painted sign: *Bluefin Florals proudly presents the 25th Annual Bluefin Bowling Banquet*. On the very top tier, the award from the mayor's office shine proudly. Each side of the award is accompanied by a retro bowling bag carrier proudly displaying the name of the league on one bag and the bowling hall on the other.

"Hello, Jackie!" a familiar female voice calls from behind me. I turn around to see Laurie calling my name. It must be her day off from the nursing home.

"Laurie!" I say, giving her a bear hug.

Laurie wiggles free. "I can't breathe!"

"I'm so sorry," I tell her. "I'm just so glad to see you."

"I missed you too!" Laurie smooths her dark chocolate brown hair, which I managed to rumple when we hugged. "I saw you standing here and thought I'd ask what you're wearing to the banquet next week?"

Whoops. I have nothing to wear and not a lot of time to buy anything. I tell Laurie, "I don't know yet. What about you?"

"I bought a blue floor-length gown from Rita's. I got it just yesterday, actually."

"Does she have any more gowns?"

"Yes, that was the second part of what I wanted to ask. There's a lavender strapless number that would look amazing on you!" Laurie pulls out here phone and says, "Look, I took a picture of the dress for you to see."

"Stunning," I admit.

"Well, if you want it, she still has time to get it fitted."

"Thanks! I'll try to get over there today."

Laurie gives me a quick hug and heads out. "I'll see you at the awards banquet!"

Candice is busy showing Dad around the shop, so on impulse I decide to head over to Rita's right away. Her store is painted pink, and when

Valentine's Day hits, her front windows are bursting with hearts and flowers. She tells everyone that pink is her signature color.

Rita opens the door to let a customer out as I walk up.

"That dress looks great on you, Shannon!" she calls. "Jackie!" she greets me with a broad smile. "What can I do for you today?"

"Laurie just showed me a picture of the most gorgeous purple dress. Please tell me you still have it!" I say, as she ushers me into the shop.

"You mean that one?" Rita asks, nodding at the dress display.

"Yes! That's the one." *I'm buying that dress no matter what.* "Can you size me up, please?"

She looks at her watch. "I can try and squeeze you in, but I have another fitting in twenty minutes." Rita removes the dress from the mannequin, and we walk over to the fitting rooms.

"Just in time for the banquet," I say, securing the latch on the door behind me. I lower the dress to my ankles and step in, then slide it up and over my chest.

Rita knocks at the door. "Step out here! Let me see ya."

I unlatch the door and Rita grabs me by the hand, leading me to the floor-length mirror. My other arm is holding the dress across my chest, trying to prevent a wardrobe malfunction.

Rita zips me up, and I can lower my arm to take in the full effect. The gown is embellished with tiny rhinestones that start at the waist and cascade down the skirt, where the purple gives way to a shining silver silk.

Rita reaches over and pulls my hair up into a messy French twist, showing me how I would look with my hair up.

"I may have to take a little in on the skirt, but the bodice is a perfect fit!" Rita starts to mark the dress with a white clothing pen. She then stands and grabs a pair of purple pumps, bringing them over to me.

I feel like a princess when she slips my feet into the slippers, but then I remember the burning airplane, when my heel got stuck in the melting floor. I shake my head to dislodge the thought. *I need to get back to Candice and Dad.*

Rita takes my order, and I wave and thank her as I head back across the street to see what Candice and Dad are up to.

"So, what do you think of your daughter's shop?" I ask him.

Dad's beaming with pride. "She's done such a great job! I couldn't have done it better myself."

"Speaking of Candice," I say, "where is she?"

"Oh, Grace needed her signature on some stuff in the back. She'll be back shortly." He shifts uncomfortably, as though he feels awkward in his castaway clothes.

"Hey, Dad, while she's doing that, do you want to get some better-fitting threads?" I ask. "My treat!"

"Can we?" he asks. "I thought you'd never ask."

I laugh and grab him by the arm to lead him away from the floral shop, yelling back to Candice so she knows where we are.

I link arms with my dad and we head back over to Rita's.

"Hey Dad," I whisper. "Everyone in Bluefin Cove thinks you're dead. If anyone should ask, you're my cousin from New York."

"I can do that," he agrees. "I guess you can't go around telling people I'm your dead father. That would *really* get the town's gossip going, huh?"

Entering the store, I wave to Rita, and we pivot to the right side for men's clothing.

"Paul?" I have to resist the urge to call him *Dad*. "What kind of clothes do you want? A suit? A T-shirt?"

"A suit for the banquet next week, that's for certain." He picks up a black blazer and tries it on, battling the price tags. "This blazer costs how much!"

"Dad." I snort. "Prices have gone up a lot since 1971. Inflation is at an all-time high. And, who cares. I am buying it for you." He challenges the offer but concedes in the end.

After an hour of looking around the store, we've picked out a nice new wardrobe for Dad. Rita looks shocked when she rings up our tab: nearly two thousand dollars, and I haven't even paid for the dress yet. *Do I even have a job? Since we changed the past, the Jenkins law office doesn't exist.*

Later on that evening, we head down to the boardwalk for dinner. Besides the Bluefin Café, we have a seafood and burger restaurant. Redondo's serves up the best seafood Mexican dishes on the east coast. During the main course, I ask Dad, "How far in the past have you time-traveled?"

His response gets our attention. "Nah, yeah, that would be April 14, 1912." He smiles and waits for us to respond.

"April 14, 1912?" Candice said. "But that's the night —"

Dad cuts her off. "The night the Titanic sank. That's right."

"Dad, you were on the ship?" I ask. "The real ship?"

"Yes, I was. Unbelievably elegant. A real masterpiece, that cruiser."

Candice takes a bit of her salad. "You didn't warn them about the iceberg?"

"I ended up arriving an hour *after* the ship collided with the iceberg. There was nothing I could do, girls. I just had to watch people and learn as much as I could until it was time to return home."

"How did you get there, Dad?" I ask, taking a sip of my tea.

He finishes chewing his steak. "I was on a layover near Southampton, and we went to a small artifact museum with the flight attendants. They had some items on display from the original ship."

"But… I thought they didn't even find the ship until 1985?" I ask, trying to call his bluff.

"They were items that people had brought home in their pockets, along with some of the lifeboats and gear. I touched one of the lifeboats and *boom*, I was on board!"

He has more stories like that — a long list of them, and he regales Candice and me with his adventures over dinner and dessert. Once we get home, Candice heads up to bed and I go to the kitchen to brew a pot of coffee.

I get two cups out of the cabinet and set them down on the counter. "How do you like your coffee?" I ask Dad, then I remember the cockpit recording — he ordered his coffee black from the flight attendant. "Black?"

He grins, watching me pour almond creamer into my own cup.

"How do you get creamer from an almond?" he asks, flummoxed.

"To be honest, Dad, I have no idea, but it tastes good, and it has less calories."

Dad takes a seat at the kitchen table, and I join him. We sit there for a moment in silence, as I try to figure out how to say what I want to say.

"Thanks for saving my life," I venture finally.

"You saved mine!" he says, warming his hands on his cup.

"I have a question, though," I say, sipping my brew. "When I touched a broken piece of the lavatory mirror, I went back to 1971 and ended up in your airplane. But, when I tried to touch the mirror a second time, it didn't work. Why not? Melinda told me all I'd have to do is touch the mirror and I'd travel right back to the present day."

Dad stiffens, and I get the feeling he's reluctant to answer my question.

"Jackie, there is no easy way to explain our gift," he says. "The government doesn't know the whole truth about it. I wanted them to think I could go just by touching a piece of the wreckage."

"That doesn't make any sense, though," I say. There's a silence. Finally, I dig deep and tell him, "Dad, I want to know everything, please."

He takes a breath like he's about to speak, but he hesitates.

I sip my coffee, trying to keep my hands occupied because I'm pretty sure they're shaking. "Dad, there's a reason why we get a second chance to know each other again. Please, help me understand this gift."

My father sighs. "Okay, Jackie, what do you want to know?"

"How did you make us time-travel off of that burning plane?"

He frowned. "I don't want to get into it right now." He hissed.

"I saw your eyes turn radiant white, and then you asked me about the date I came from."

He changes the subject numerous times, and I give up on learning about who he is and who I am. We spend the rest of the night with him telling me more about the voyages, the different places and the times he's been to, and the trauma he's seen along the way. We only stop talking when the sunrise peeks above the horizon, lighting up the white lace curtains in the kitchen.

CHAPTER 14

The next week passes with no further conversations about time travel, since Dad and I are helping Candice get ready for the Bowling League banquet. Two days before the big night, Rita calls to let me know my dress is ready for pickup, and Candice drives me into town to try it on.

"Rita?" I call out when we get there. "Rita?"

Finally, she appears from the back room, laboring under a stack of cardboard boxes.

"Jackie! Hi! Can I get a hand?" I take the boxes and follow her instructions for where they should go. Then I notice she's already getting the witch costumes ready for Halloween.

"Never too early, huh?" I ask. Rita knows what I'm here for, and she's already pulling out another box with my order.

"I know it seems early to set up the October window display, but if I don't, then people go shop somewhere else, and I lose the sale. As soon as the Bowling League banquet is finished, I'm full speed ahead on Halloween."

Rita unboxes the purple dress and whips it from the box, holding it up in front of me. The soft, silky folds ripple to the ground. *It's even more beautiful than I remembered.* I'm so happy I got it before someone else could.

I head over to the dressing room to try it on. While I'm stepping into the dress, Rita slides a box with my new shoes under the door. "Put these on and come out to the mirrors."

"Okay, one sec!" I reply.

Everything's a perfect fit. I emerge from the small dressing room, holding up the front of the gown so I don't step on it.

"Wow!" Rita says. "Let me see! Let me see!"

I give Rita a small twirl like I did with Stephanie's red dress in Washington, and then she holds out her hand to help me up on the platform. I let go of the dress, mesmerized by my glamorous reflection.

"Is everything alright, Jackie?"

I take a moment to respond. "Rita, I have no words. This dress is... incredible." She's has taken in the sides just like she said she would, and now it fits like a second skin.

"Well, that's not *all* my hard work." Rita says, bending down to fluff out the bottom of the dress.

"What do you mean?"

"I had to enlist the help of my mother in order to add a blind stitch." Rita says.

"How is Dorothy doing?" I haven't seen her since the bowling banquet last year.

"Good. When she gets bored in her retirement, I ask her to help me with a *tough* sew. It's not that I need the help, but my asking for help makes her feel needed," Rita says.

We reminisce shortly, then I head for the dressing room. While I change back into my old clothes, Rita takes the dress and folds it carefully so it won't wrinkle inside the box. Finally, I pay her an arm and a leg so she'll let me take my fabulous new outfit home.

Later that evening, Candice tells me she'll be wearing one of her birth mother's dresses to the banquet.

"Amazing! Can I see?"

"Oh, that's right! I didn't tell you about the suitcase," Candice says. Over the next few minutes, Candice tells me all about exploring her birth parents' belongings in that long-forgotten suitcase, and about the beautiful dresses that Melinda let her keep.

"Well, where is it?" I ask. "I want to see it!"

We race up the stairs like a couple of teenage girls. Heading for Candice's room, I see a black garment bag handing on the closest door. *Funny, I don't remember seeing that yesterday.* She pulls it off the door and lays it on the bed.

"What are you waiting for?" I ask. "Try it on!"

Candice removes her clothes down to her undergarments, talking to me as she changes. "I know it's vintage, but it's the most sentimental item I own now. And I have two of them!"

Candice finally emerges, modeling a gorgeous dress that's patterned with red and pink roses. "Stephanie took in the sides and added a slimmer thing to the middle." She does a little twirl for me, and the skirt flares out prettily.

"When did you have time for *that*?" I ask.

She slips off the dress and packs it back in the garment bag. "She was able to do it while you were on your trip back in time." She shakes her head, giggling. "We even had a girl night at the office with Chinese food."

"Glad to hear you had fun while I was risking my life in a plane crash," I tell her.

Candice rolls her eyes. "You're so dramatic, sis."

Two days later, the big night arrives. Candice and I start out the day at the beauty salon. My sister has her hair done in a soft and romantic updo, with a small bun at the nape of her neck. Mine is half French twist, half braided cascades. With my strapless dress, it's perfect.

That evening, Candice comes down in her mother's pearl necklace and dress, looking breathtaking. I feel my mouth drop as she arrives at the base of the stairs. "Wow, Candice you are so beautiful." I smiled.

Dad emerges from his room, looking very sharp in his black blazer. He comes to a complete stop when he sees Candice in her brilliant dress. Only seconds later, a tear rolls down his cheek.

"What's wrong?" I ask, noticing his red eyes.

"I had always wondered what the two of you would look like all grown up, and I am so proud of you both," he beams, turning his attention to my dress, which I had covered with a dark purple overcoat.

"What are you wearing?" He asks me.

I unbutton the cloak and remove it, displaying my beautiful dress.

"I can't believe that I am here, witnessing my two grown daughters attend a party in the most beautiful dresses." He wipes another tear from his eye.

The three of us link arms and pile into a rented limo that I've arranged as a surprise. This is the biggest event of the season, and I want to make sure we go in style.

The town hall looks very grand for Bluefin Cove. As we step out of the car, I gaze up at the three-story red-brick building. The four large columns in front provide a grand entrance, and a red carpet is rolled out for this evening's event.

"Wow, this is just for a bowling banquet?" Dad asks as we walk up the steps and into the building.

"Yes, we really only do an event like this twice a year in Bluefin," Candice tells him. We head for the photo booth where the background is a similar arrangement to the window display that Candice and Grace had created in her shop. Numerous couples take their photos while we wait our turn.

The photographer is Timmy Wilkins. He was the student council photographer through middle school and high school. Timmy was in charge of school pictures as well as the team sports photos.

"Hi, Timmy!" Candice bubbled. We find our pose, and Timmy straightens us out.

"Okay, ready? 1, 2, 3." Two flashes burst, and our photo is captured. Timmy points out that he will have them in his shop in a few days.

"I'll swing by to pick them up." Candice coquettishly "It will be good to see you again."

After the photo op, I break away to sign us all in with the guest book. The foyer is filled with excitement and lots of flowers. The dining tables are covered in white linen, with bowling ball vases and a mix of flowers.

The dance floor is crowded with people dancing and enjoying themselves. Dad and Candice are boogeying right out in the middle. Our table is next to the stage, and I take a seat by all the trophies. The next thing I know, Laurie plops down next to me in a bright yellow dress that hangs off both of her shoulders. The top of the dress is bright yellow lace, and she's wearing matching heels. I bet she spent more on the dress than her car payment for a year.

"Who is that handsome man dancing with your sister?" Laurie asks, just now noticing them on the dance floor. She called Dad *handsome.* Laurie has been divorced for a year and just turned forty.

"Oh, he's our cousin, Paul, from New York," I say. "He's staying with us for a few weeks to see if he wants to move here."

"I didn't know you had a cousin in New York. Is he single?" she asks promiscuously, shimming her shoulders.

"Recently widowed," I giggle, which is probably the wrong emotion, but Laurie doesn't know the truth. "He's been through a lot and needs a change of pace." Laurie nods. *Plus,* I think to myself, *that's not a lie.*

"It's too bad we can't time-travel to a happier time in our lives," she muses.

"Oh Laurie," I sigh. "If you only knew."

A gentleman in a tuxedo gets up on stage. "Dinner is served," he announces into the mic. We stand to head for the buffet line. Even though we're dressed for dinner on Park Avenue, the Bowling League still serves buffet style to save money on waitstaff. Instead, our community development group lets teenagers complete their volunteer hours by helping out at the banquet.

Candice meets me in line with dad accompanying her. "Dad has some good dance moves," she whispers careful not to bring attention by the surrounding attendees, grabbing her plate.

"Oh, he does, does he? Guess he'll have to prove that after dinner." I nudge my father playfully in the ribs.

The main course is a choice between chicken tikka masala, made from delicious boneless chicken chunks marinated in tomato puree, coconut cream, and a masala spice mix, or an Atlantic salmon with a generous lacquer of spiced maple glaze. A generous selection of vegetables is offered as side to the main dishes, from caramelized carrots to thick, gravy-covered mashed potatoes.

Personally, I'm excited for the dessert bar. There's a chocolate fountain with a whole bunch of fruits and small cakes to dip. They also are serving chocolate chip cookies in mini cast iron skillets — donated by Russ Hartman who owns the town's only auto mechanic, Bluefin Motors.

Each iron skillet serves two and is a thank-you gift, which the guests can take home. On the back of the skillet is a beautiful depiction of our town logo with a *present by Bluefin Motors Since 1955* on the bottom.

Once we finish our dinner and before I can grab dessert, I take my father's hand. "Come on, Dad, let's see how your 1970s dance moves hold up in 2023." He laughs and follows me around the maze of tables that lead to the dance floor.

Once we find some space, he places his hands on my lower back, and I link mine around his neck. A waltz begins to play, and together we dance in perfect sync.

He twirls me like a ballerina, and we spin across the floor, then back again. The song comes to an end and without even thinking about it, we give each other a big hug.

Our hug is interrupted when Laurie leans in. "Wow, Jackie! Your cousin sure knows how to spin you and Candice around."

"Why, thank you," Dad says with a little bow, then he turns and walks away.

"Paul, where are you going?" I call.

"I'll be right back!" He approaches the disc jockey and whispers in his ear. The DJ nods, and Dad comes back to me.

"What are you doing?" I ask.

"I'm going to show you how we get down in my world," he grins. Five seconds later, a pulsing beat starts playing.

"Oh yeah," Dad says with a glint in his eye. "This is a great dancing song." He sings along: "I took my troubles down to Madame Ruth."

He grabs my hand again and twirls me. "Sellin' little bottles of Love Potion Number Nine."

Once the song finishes and the crowd claps, a deep male voice starts to sing and give commands. The people surrounding us stand silent, as most of them haven't heard this song in decades... and the young people have *never* heard it.

Dad leads, following the singer's commands by twisting his body back and forth and then completely a spin and back again. I join in and soon after, I see Laurie and her date for the evening, a doctor of course, venture in. Then Shannon, Frank, and more join us. By the end of the song, we have at least forty people dancing on the dance floor.

When the song ends completely, everyone claps and yells, "Bravo!" Dad bows elaborately to the assembled group.

"What song was that?" I ask.

"What! You've never heard of The Twist by Chubby Checker?" He says. I shake my head with a giggle to follow.

A new song comes on, and we go back to our modern pop songs, but it's not too long before dessert is announced and served.

Candice and I load up on our plates from the dessert bar.

"Boy, these chocolate-covered strawberries are *huge!*" I say to Shannon, who's a sweaty mess after her whirl on the dance floor.

"I know, and they're super-fresh. They got them from Molly's fruit stand," Shannon replies. "You remember Molly, right? She was the one we voted least likely to succeed in school."

"I do!" I say. "And I also heard she sold over ten thousand bushels this year so far."

"How does she manage to coordinate her work at the senior home with such a busy farm?" Candice asks.

Shannon rolls her eyes. "Well, as a matter of fact, that loser ex-boyfriend of hers came through town earlier this month and wanted to get back together as soon as he found out she got the five-hundred-acre farm business in the will."

We all know Molly would never get back with him. I try to change the subject, but right then, Molly arrives at our table. "Hey, you guys!" she greets us. "Enjoying the strawberries?"

"*Amazing,*" I tell her. "And you look radiant today. Is that a new dress?" She's in great shape, and she's had no work done. *Must be all that healthy living on the farm!*

"Thanks!" Then she lowers her voice. "I found it in a shop in Portland." Pressing a finger to her lips, she whispers, "Shh, don't tell Rita. She'll never forgive me."

"And who's this handsome young man on your arm?" Candice asks.

The tall, fair-haired gentleman at her side extends his hand. "Evening," he says. "I'm Tyler."

"He owns the distribution plant in Portland," Molly explains. "We met during a seminar at his company last month. Aaaaand…" She raises her left hand and displays a beautiful diamond ring. "We got married yesterday!"

We all scream like schoolgirls, congratulating the happy couple.

I pull in her hand to take a closer look. "Careful when you go swimming," I joke. "That rock'll drag you to the bottom of the ocean if you're not wearing a life vest."

"Did you change your name?" Candice asks, leaning in for the gossip.

"Yes!" Molly's eyes shine with happiness. "It's Fletcher, like the Fletcher Farms in Portland."

We all chat for a few minutes longer, then an announcement comes over the loudspeaker. "Ladies and gentlemen, if you would please take your seats. The Bluefin Bowling League is proud to present this year's winners."

Some of the teenage volunteers bring the brilliantly polished trophies out onto the stage. The championship prize is a whopper that takes two kids to carry it: a six-foot-tall trophy with bowling pins as columns and an eagle at the very top. The top of the trophy is engraved with the names of the winning team members.

A woman announcer approaches the mic in a blue sequined dress.

"Ladies and gentlemen, I want to thank you all, on behalf of the town committee, for being here tonight." We all clap, and she continues. "I know it's been a very competitive season, especially with Carl and Max battling it out since December."

The crowd laughs. We all know that Carl and Max Johnson are brothers who love each other to death, but they also compete on different bowling teams. Once the crowd calms down, the speaker continues, "It is my pleasure to announce that our champions for the 2022-2023 bowling year are… no other than… The Bluefin Sailors!"

The hall echoes with resounding applause. Just as the team walks up to the stage to accept their trophy and pose for a photo with the mayor, I feel a tap on my shoulder. I turn around, expecting to see someone from Bluefin Cove, but to my surprise, it's Agent Taylor.

He bends over and whispers, "I need you and Paul to follow me."

I shoot a confused look at Dad. *I thought Melinda gave us a month off?* Nevertheless, I place my napkin on the table, and the two of us stand.

"Will you all please excuse us?" I voice to the other guests around our table. Following Agent Taylor, we exit the ballroom and proceed down the hallway.

Halfway down the hall, I whisper to Dad, "What could he want at this time of night?" Dad just shrugs his shoulders, and we continue following Agent Taylor, who stops at the end of the long hallway. The hallway to the left goes into the mayor's offices and the right side heads to the file room.

He turns to us. "I'm so sorry to pull you out of your party."

"What's wrong?" I ask, noting the worried look on his face.

"There's been a development. Melinda needs both of you to come to the office right away."

"What about Candice?" I ask.

"I already sent a text to her phone. She'll be okay."

"What's the nature of the situation?" Dad wants to know. "Jenkins always briefed me up front."

"Well, I'm not him," Agent Taylor replies brusquely. "It's a matter of national security that I can't repeat in a public space. We'll go to my car. This way." He turns to the right and takes off down the hall away from the other guests. Dad and I try to keep up.

"Hey, I'm in heels!" I shout indignantly. "And they're not the ones Stephanie designed." But Agent Taylor just quickens his pace, gesturing at me to speed up.

Once we're in the car on our way to Jette Industries, Agent Taylor starts to explain. "Melinda received a classified document about an hour ago."

"Okay, can you narrow that down a bit?" I ask. "Just spit it out! For heaven's sake." I'm not feeling particularly patient, since he made us leave the banquet and abandon my sister in the bargain.

"Paul, there's been an accident. I'm so sorry to tell you this, but Mr. Jenkins was killed about two hours ago in a crash outside of Louisville." Agent Taylor's face looks grim.

"What kind of crash?" Dad asks. He looks devastated. Of course, Dad knew him better than anyone. Even though I had worked for the man for more than 20 years, I had hardly known him besides being my boss. Our relationship never extended beyond that, and now I know why.

"The only other information I have, sir, is that the aircraft went down twenty minutes before landing."

"Will Melinda have more details?" I ask, placing my hand on my dad's knee to comfort him.

"Yes, Melinda has the full briefing."

The remainder of the drive is quiet, the only noise the soft hum of the tires on the road. At the airfield, we're met with armed guards at the gate. Agent Taylor displays his badge, and they let us through. Navigating the tarmac and airport service roads, he brings us to the building for Jette Industries.

When we pull up to the main entrance, Melinda is standing outside.

"Melinda?" Dad asks. "What do we know about the crash?"

"Let's head inside and talk in my office," she says. She ushers us all into the building. In her office, we sit down at the big conference table. She has a file already on the tabletop in a red folder. *Uh-oh,* I think. *That means we have an assignment.*

Opening the folder, Melinda says, "Here's what we know." She flips the paper around to Dad, and he scans its contents. "The aircraft that went down was a NorthJet Airways Boeing 737-700 series," she tells us. "The plane was on its final approach into Louisville Airport in Kentucky. The pilot's last radio transmission to the tower was '*Mayday, mayday, mayday. This is NorthJet 4145. We have an engine fire in the number two, requesting emergency services to meet us on the taxiway.*' The next event was impact."

Dad grunts in acknowledgment. "And Jenkins?"

Melinda pulls another paper from the folder to show us. "This is the manifest from the airline. Once the NTSB was made aware of the list, a colleague forwarded it to me. I reviewed it myself, and his name is on it."

"He could have missed the flight," I suggest.

"I'm waiting for confirmation from my colleague and the medical examiner. That will come late tomorrow."

"So, what can we do?" I ask, thinking, *why did you pull us out of the party if there's nothing happening until tomorrow?*

"Unfortunately, there's not a lot to do at this time. The main reason I had Agent Taylor pick you up tonight was due to the high security of the case and the classified information that Mr. Jenkins is aware of."

"Can you explain your concern?" I ask, because something's obviously bothering her.

"I'm concerned that this is more than just an accident. NorthJet has a radiant safety record. This is their first crash in over six decades. Until we know all the facts, I want to keep this our top priority and keep it classified."

We discuss for another hour, then Melinda asks if we can come back in on Monday morning to check for updates. Personally, I'm delighted to go home and get out of my dress. I've already pulled off my heels.

Sure enough, on Monday morning Agent Taylor picks us up at 10 a.m. sharp. Candice, who spent all day Saturday recovering from the party, is delighted not to join us. I think that she wants some alone time.

Back at the office, Melinda doesn't have any new information on the crash, but she takes the opportunity to debrief us from our trip, considering all of the time off she permitted for dad to spend with Candice and I.

"Let's go over the 1971 case and close it up for good," Melinda says, pulling out the relevant files. "Since both of you disappeared after the plane landed in Halifax, these questions have gone unanswered for many years."

"Well, I was in the first-class cabin, and I witnessed no blast or explosion. When the decompression happened, though, it felt like a tornado," I say.

"The only alarm that sounded in the cockpit was the loss of pressure," Dad adds.

"According to radar," Melinda states, "You had already put the aircraft into a steep dive. The recording from air traffic control, since the black box burned in the fire, said '*Pan Pan Pan, we are in grave and immediate danger. We are descending through flight level three-one-zero.*'"

"That is correct," Dad confirms. "When Jackie advised me something would happen, I knew that our best chance was to get to a breathable altitude and prepare my crew for the worst."

"The investigators assigned to the crash documented a large hole in the rear cabin, noticed by numerous emergency personnel," Melinda reads from the file.

"Did we lose any passengers?" Dad asks.

"No, sir," Melinda says proudly. "Everyone but you and a mysterious woman, in a red dress, survived the emergency landing."

"What did they find after the fire?" Dad asks.

"It burned so hot, most of the aircraft was lost. Only metal that could withstand the tremendous heat survived," Melinda replies.

"Were any of the passengers in the rear cabin interviewed?" I ask.

"Yes, all the passengers were interviewed. In the summary report, there is a mention of three passengers, in seats 19E, 19F and 20C, who all reported an alarm sounding just before the explosion occurred."

"Where did the alarm come from? Which direction in the aircraft?" Dad asks.

Melinda looks down at the document. "The summary report does not specify."

"Jackie says the cabin became a whirlwind of debris. That tells me the cabin had a large enough hole for items to be sucked out."

Something isn't adding up. My gut is telling me we need to look further into this.

"Melinda? Since I didn't follow your orders, the passengers survived, right?" She nods her head. "Do we have testimonies from every passenger and crew member?"

"Yes," she replies, pulling out another file. This one is labeled *Passenger Testimonies.*

"Well, let's get started," I say, pulling the file toward me. "We know that the front of the cabin was unaffected by the blast, but what do the flight attendant testimonies say?"

Sifting through the files, Melinda pulls out the flight attendants' reports and displays them on the table. I rummage over the files until I locate Marge's.

"Ah ha!" I pull her file and open it.

"What? Did you find something already?" Melinda asks.

"Not yet," I say. "I had a lot of communication with Marge on the flight, and I want to see what she said in her testimony." I lift the cover and display the report's first page. Marge's testimony fills numerous pages.

I peruse the report, and everything matches with what I witnessed. I want to know if she saw the hole or whatever was in the rear cabin. On the third page, she remarked, *Assisting Gail in row 20, we moved injured passengers away from the hole.* When asked to describe the damage to the aircraft, she said, *the hole was the size of a suitcase below the window with insulation swaying in the wind as the air passed over and under the wing. The sound coming from the engine was abnormal.*

"Hey, Dad?" I mutter. He turns his attention to me while he reads the first officer's report. "Did Marge say anything about the engines sounding *abnormal*?"

"Yes, she called the cockpit just before I made the final descent announcement."

"What did she say?" I ask.

He looks towards the ceiling, trying to remember her exact words. "She called and said that the engine was surging. After her call, I instructed the flight engineer to shut down the engine."

Marge does not mention anything else about the damage. I move on to the next flight attendant, one from the rear cabin. Gail's report is only two pages in length. I open it and review. *Immediately after we unbuckled from our jump seats, I walked through the entire cabin on the way up to Judy for medical supplies. While in route, my arm was grabbed by a customer in row 20. Seat D.*

I continue reading the report and then announce to everyone when I find something interesting. "When I looked down at the man who grabbed my arm, my arms were drawn to the small hole in the wall by seat 20F. I watched as the hole grew from the size of a purse to the size of a suitcase."

Closing the folder, I ask. "How did the hole grow if the cabin pressure was equal, Dad?"

"It could have been a variety of things. The skin on an aircraft exterior is thin. Compare it to a paper clip. When you bend and bend and bend, the clip breaks. The exterior just gave way until it met a row of rivets under the window."

"When I was in the cabin, there were no noises or abnormal sounds prior to the blast," I say, trying to find the missing piece. "Melinda? Do any of the files you've reviewed over the past years state anything about the noise before the blast?"

"When Ken and I reviewed the files before he retired, there was no mention of sounds before, other than the summary report," she answered, only leading to more questions. Ken was a professional. Surely, he would have noticed something.

"Well, we have no choice." File by file and seat by seat, we start reviewing each passenger's statement. All of the testimonies here, have no written documentation about anything amiss before the blasts.

I lean back in my chair, thinking.

"What's wrong?" Melinda asks.

"Something's missing," I tell her.

"No, these are all the files we have."

I can't help but feel that there are fewer files than we should have. I go through the pages again, one at a time.

"Can I see the original manifest?" I ask.

She hands it to me. I slide a stack of passenger testimonies over to Dad and Melinda. "Start calling out seat numbers to me," I say. I pick up a marker from the table, removing the cap.

They do, and which each seat number they call out, I cross it off on the manifest. After ten minutes of calling out the names, I arrive at a grim conclusion.

"Look," I say, turning the paper around so they can both read it. "Do you see what I see?"

"Hey, there are no Xs on row 20 of the first officer's starboard side," Melinda observes. We all know the manifest clearly states that seats 20D, 20E, and 20F were occupied by passengers.

"Can we cross-check the names in your database, Melinda?" I'm wondering if they'll pop up in any terrorist organizations.

She turns to her computer. "What's the first name?"

"Robert Fritzel, seat 20D," I tell her.

"Clean, nothing comes up."

"If nothing comes up in your database, then where's his file?" I ask. "Who had access to these files after the incident?"

"Numerous people," she shrugs.

"Okay, well, that doesn't help. Let's keep going with the names. Next person is John Townsend, seat 20E."

This search takes a little longer than before. "Okay, he had a few warrants for robbery and possession, but nothing that would make me believe he could bring down a jet," Melinda reports.

I read out the final name. "Seat 20F, Dustin Bluwood." Melinda enters it in her computer.

"Nothing," she replies. "Nothing on him at all."

"I just don't get it," I shake my head. "What are we missing?" I scan the manifest again, passenger seat by passenger seat.

Melinda's phone rings, and she answers it. "Uh-huh...uh-huh...okay, thank you." She hangs up and turns back to us. "Well, that was my colleague with information from the medical examiner at the crash site," she says. "We now have the confirmation that Mr. Jenkins was indeed on the flight."

"What do we do now?" I ask. I find it hard to believe that Mr. Jenkins was on that plane by coincidence, considering that he had his own private jet. *What was he doing flying to Louisville, anyway?*

"Dad?" I ask, "Have you ever heard of Mr. Jenkins going to Kentucky... like ever?"

"No, and come to think of it, he had no family west of New York." He replies.

"Do you think he was forced on the flight?"

"I think it's worth finding out. Considering that three files are missing and Jenkins took an abnormal flight, it's more than a coincidence." Dad answers.

Melinda nods in agreement. She turns and leans over to her intercom and says, "Sally, will you get Stephanie in here, please."

"What are you doing? And why do we need outfits for a more present time?" I ask.

"I want you both to travel back to yesterday and be on that plane. I'll have to fly us out there tomorrow and look for a piece of debris that will get you both inside of the cabin prior to impact." Melinda states. "As far as the outfit, I don't want to mess up your own clothes, and I want you both to be in an outfit designed by Stephanie for every mission." This is the first orderly command she has given today.

My heart beats hard in my chest. "Dad, are you game?"

"Absolutely!" he responds. "I need to find out why an older man would fly with the general public when he has a private plane."

Stephanie barges through the door a few moments later and asks us to come with her. She takes us to separate dressing rooms. "Hang on!" I hear her shout.

"You're not giving me heels again, are you?" I ask nervously.

She slides a garment bag over the door, and I hear her give one to Dad. "You should both find these outfits a bit more comfortable."

The garment pouch unzips easily, and I'm relieved to see normal clothing. There's a black blazer with a white button-up blouse and matching black pants. Slipping off my clothes, I put on the outfit. It's comfortable and easy to move in, *thank goodness.*

Once I emerge from the fitting room, Stephanie adjusts my blazer. "Perfect!" she says with satisfaction.

"Can you make all of my future outfits feel this nice?" I ask.

"Depends on when you travel," she shrugs. "This was an easy project and a quick one. Usually, Melinda gives me some time to create — but this was a fast fix."

I step up to the platform and mirror and admire how professional I look. Dad then emerges from his dressing room in a polo and beige dress pants.

"Is this a business flight?" I ask. My dad and I both look like lawyers in these getups.

"Yes, according to Melinda, the flight originated in Washington, at Reagan National."

"Everything okay, Mr. Jette?" Stephanie asks, noticing my dad frowning down at his clothes.

"This is what businessmen wear in 2023?" he asks critically. "No suit and tie?"

Stephanie smiles. "No, sir, this is what 90 percent of American businesspeople wear when they travel."

She turns back to me. "Now, Melinda wants you both to leave right away. So here are a few crash course tips." She pauses. "No pun intended."

Indicating our outfits, she gives us our briefing. "These don't have lights or radio beacons in them like the dress you wore to 1971 or Paul like you wore on Ocean crossing flights. Since the crash site is still active, there was no reason to add them in as people will be there. Also, if you look in your pockets, you'll find cell phones and paper boarding passes."

Dad and I pull out our boarding passes. To me, they look standard, but Dad seems confused. "Why do we need paper boarding passes?" I ask.

"Business travelers never trust a phone that could glitch after the three major airlines had technology issues a few Christmases ago. Always have a backup." She beams.

"Question, Mr. Jette?" Stephanie asks.

"What's my seat number?" He points to the boarding position on the paper pass. "What does this mean?"

"Oh, that's right. You haven't flown on today's jets." Stephanie explains, "On this airline, there are no assigned seats. You sit wherever you want after the boarding pass is scanned."

Once we get Dad up to speed, Stephanie completes our outfits with shoes, jewelry, watches and more. A private jet is waiting for us on the tarmac just in front of the hangar. Agent Taylor and Melinda accompany us on our quick trip to Louisville.

When we taxi out to the runway, the pilots advise us that the flight time should be a quick one hour and twenty minutes. I am still amazed at how this once-abandoned airfield is now an operational organization… *but I guess that's time travel for you.*

At cruising altitude, we have a briefing with Melinda at the small conference table in the cabin. "Here's the plan," Melinda begins. "I want you and Jackie to locate a piece of wreckage with Agent Taylor. YOU do not touch a single piece. You will point, and he will pick it up for further review."

"That seems prudent," Dad observes.

Melinda continues. "Once you locate a piece that you can confirm is from the interior of the cabin, you will both travel to the same place, but not together."

"Like, Dad would go first, then I would go next?" I ask.

"That's correct," Melinda confirms. "Once you're both on board the airplane, you will only have limited time, depending on which phase of the flight you arrive in. Hopefully, it will be enough."

"Are we looking for anything in particular?" Dad asks.

We spend the rest of the flight in silence. Dad keeps looking out the windows and mumbling under his breath that the pilot should be doing this and that. I giggle as I have seen the dad vibe on funny internet videos, and now here I am. "No backseat flying!" I shout and chuckle.

Before Dad can respond, the pilots ring us on the public address system to announce our landing. As we make our final approach, we fly directly over the crash site. The field is black with burnt debris and grass.

"Whoa," Dad remarks. "They must have hit the ground very hard. It looks more like a campfire pit than the remains of a jet."

After landing and a quick taxi, a car picks us up at the plane and transports us to the wreck site. The stench is awful — like a gas station mingled with rotting meat in the trash can. Tears burst from my eyes and run down my cheeks. The site is so gruesome. Clothes, shoes, seat frames with cushions still attached and other items spread out and singed. All of it soaked in jet fuel. A single off-white high heel catches my gaze. *That was someone's shoe and had planned on wearing them again.*

The only identifiable parts of the aircraft are a section of windows and a chunk of the tail. I stand there for a few moments, staring at the windows.

"Jackie?" Dad says touching my elbow. "What are you thinking?

"Dad, do you ever think about who was looking through those just before they were killed? Looking at the beautiful scenery, just knowing they were going to die and there was nothing that they could do about it?"

"I used to think about that when I first started, but now I treat it more like a job. I just try to remember my purpose for being there."

"What do you mean, purpose?"

"Some planes have to crash, so that aviation becomes safer for future generations," he answers. "Every crash that I've investigated led to safety improvements that save the lives of millions of people."

I think about his words, continuing to inspect the crash site for usable items.

"What about the windows?" I say, pointing at the same row.

"Never touch the windows," he commands.

"Why?"

"Because, while the window will get you there, how do you know which one will bring you back?"

His statement fuels the question burning in my head.

"Agent Taylor?" Dad says suddenly, pointing. "Would you please pick that piece up?" Agent Taylor does so, holding it up so Dad can take a closer look.

It's a small mechanical fragment that means nothing to me.

"What is that, Dad?"

"It looks like a piece of the flight deck control." He squints at it. "It's the speed indicator gauge. Agent Taylor, would you please tilt it just a little more?"

"Sure," Agent Taylor says, angling the piece to the side.

"That's what I wanted to see."

"What is it, Dad?"

"Jackie, look. See that mark indented on the back?"

I look closer and see what he's talking about. "Is that how fast the aircraft was traveling when it hit the ground?"

"Yep." Dad frowns. "An approach speed should be anywhere between 150 and 170 knots when coming in for a landing."

The indent is at the 200 knot mark. "Why were they going so darned *fast?*"

My dad looks determined. "I'm not sure, but we're going to find out."

Agent Taylor places the indicator in a clear plastic evidence bag. We continue searching, though the terrain is rocky and uneven from the impact.

Dad breaks away, his attention focused on an item off to the side. Something else draws my eye, but when I try to approach it, my foot catches a piece of debris and I fall face-first into the dirt.

"Jackie!" Dad shouts. "Are you okay?" He and Agent Taylor run over to help me up.

"Yes, I'm fine." I tell them. "Just humiliated." I look around and start to get to my feet. I grab a large piece of aluminum to balance myself.

"Jackie! No!" Dad yells.

CHAPTER 15

"Ladies and gentlemen, as you may have noticed, we have begun our initial descent into the Louisville airport. At this time, we're going to swing by and pick up any remaining service items or trash in preparation for landing. Please return any carry-on items to their proper storage locations, and raise your seatbacks and tray tables to their upright and locked positions. Thank you for your attention, and welcome to Louisville."

My heart is racing faster than a freight train downhill as I have no idea how to get back on my own. *Dam, I wished I would have watched where I was stepping.* I still there and start observing my surrounds trying to calm myself.

It's a light flight, as I don't see many heads popping up behind the seats. *Thank God for that.* Luckily, the piece I touched happened to be part of a seat frame at the rear of the cabin, where no one can see me. *I'd hate to think what would have happened if I'd touched the engine block.*

The window shade beside me is closed. I reach over and lift it, revealing a delicate scattering of wispy clouds. Far below, I can see patches of small towns and bright green farmland. The tip of the wing and winglet aren't bouncing at all. So far, the flight is perfectly calm.

I hear a flight attendant's stern voice. "Sir, please return to your seat as we're landing."

"My apologies. When you gotta go, you gotta go."

Dad? I whip my head around to confirm, and sure enough, my dad's standing right outside the toilets. I wave to him, motioning for him to take a seat by me.

Dad sits down and whispers, "Jackie, why did you take off like that? You scared me."

"Like it was my choice!" I hiss back. "I was just trying to stand up!"

"We'll talk about this later. For now, we have to figure out what Mr. Jenkins is doing on this plane." Dad cranes his head to peer around the cabin. "We need a distraction." Then he looks at me and smiles.

"What?" I ask, getting worried.

"I need you to make a fuss in the rear of the aircraft and distract the flight attendants, so I can get up from my seat and have a private conversation with Mr. Jenkins."

"Okay… and what do you want me to do?" Honestly, I prefer to blend in with the crowd. Candice would have been the better choice for this assignment.

He ponders for a moment and looks back toward the rear galley. "I need you to try and open the door."

"You want me to do *what?*" I splutter. "What if I get sucked out?"

"The cabin is pressurized, Jackie. The door cannot physically open while under pressure." *Okay, that's reassuring. Kind of.* "And you won't pull up on the handle, just wrap your fingers around it and bend your elbows to pretend that you're opening the door."

"There has to be another option," I protest.

"Jackie, just do it!"

I take a deep breath and my heart pounds in my chest. Dad winks at me, but I don't feel confident at all. Leaving the comfort of my seat, I head for the rear galley. It's a lot smaller than I thought it would be — just enough room to make drinks and snacks. The male flight attendant is facing the rear counter, discarding used cups and soda cans.

Taking a deep breath, I scream.

The flight attendant jumps and drops his cans, then whirls around, frightened at the sudden noise.

"I want out!" I yell, and run for the door, wrapping my fingers around it like Dad instructed. I even smack the door with my palm.

"Don't touch that door!" the flight attendant yells.

Grabbing the intercom, he announces, "Code 7, rear galley." Then I feel his hands grab my shoulders with painful force.

"Get off me!" I shout, wriggling in his grip.

"Penny! Help me restrain her!" he yells.

"Ma'am, *please*," a second flight attendant pleads with me. "We're landing now, please, you will be on the ground in *just a moment*." I look down for a moment and see the same off-white-colored heels that I saw earlier at the crash site. The airlines uniform heels are the same ones. I feel sad for just a second, then get back to my mission.

I have no idea what's happening at the front of the cabin, but just like on that first flight, I know I cannot let these people die. I have to tell them. *I have to give them a fighting chance.*

I stop resisting, release the door handle, and turn. The attendants both look shocked at my sudden calm. "I'm sorry about that, but I needed to get your attention quickly."

"Why?" Penny asks.

Taking a deep breath, I say, "The number two engine is going to catch fire and cause a domino effect with the fuel line. The end result is this aircraft will crash, killing everyone on board."

"What, are you psychic?" Penny scoffs. "There's no way you could know something like that before it happens."

"Or she has something to do with it," the male flight attendant adds.

"Then you have nothing to lose, right?" I tell Penny. "At least tell the captain about it, and have him shut down the engine as a precaution."

The two flight attendants look at me, then at each other. Penny walks over to the interphone.

"Captain, we have a disgruntled passenger in the rear galley. She's demanding that you shut down the number two engine to prevent an explosion or fire." There's a pause, and Penny sighs. "I know, I know, captain, but she claims that the engine is going to explode and the fire will spread through the fuel line."

Penny hangs up the phone. "What's your name?"

"Jackie, Jackie Jette, NTSB." I tell her. *But is that true? Who do I work for, anyway?*

"NTSB?" the flight attendants say simultaneously, then look at each other. Two bells sound and a red light illuminates on the rear galley ceiling.

Penny returns to the phone and says, "Rear galley, this is Penny." After a brief pause, she says, "Roger, thank you, captain. Also, she says she is from the NTSB. Her name is Jackie Jette. If she was a hijacker, then why would she help us?"

Twisting her body toward me, she asks. "Do you have any ID or a badge?" I shake my head, and she replies no to the captain.

She places the phone on its port. "Okay, Jackie, I hope you're for real. He's going to follow your command, and we'll be met by emergency responders on the ground."

Her words are cut off by the captain, whose voice comes over the public address system. "Ladies and Gentlemen, this is your captain speaking. As we make our final descent into Louisville, we have had a mechanical issue, and the number two engine has been shut down. That takes care of the problem, and that engine no longer poses an issue. You will see fire and rescue approach the aircraft when we come to a complete stop, but that's just for an inspection. Please, do not be alarmed by this. We appreciate your patience and understanding."

"Ma'am, I need you to return to your seat and fasten your seatbelt." Penny says, giving me a wary look. She's still not sure if she should believe me.

I take a nearby empty seat, craning my head to see what's happening up front. I think I can make out Dad's head, next to that of an older gentleman in row 4 or 5.

The landing is smooth and uneventful. *I think I might have saved everyone's life here.* On the other hand, I went against Melinda's command not to be the hero. *Too bad,* I think. *It's worth it.*

BOOM! BOOM!

Two gunshots blast through the cabin, and the passengers yell and scream as a fight breaks out up forward. I unbuckle my belt and push my way to the front of the cabin. The aircraft screeches to a halt, nearly throwing me off my feet and onto the cabin floor. *Why me again? Why do I keep falling today?* I pick myself up, and a third gunshot rings out.

I freeze, terrified, and see a bullet hole in the ceiling. Up forward, I see Dad yank the gun away from Mr. Jenkins, and a fourth shot rings out. Mr. Jenkins slumps over instantly.

"DAD!" I call out desperately. "Are you okay?"

I scramble to his side, but my dad seems perfectly calm. He lays the pistol on the empty seat beside him, then bends down to pick up a black leather briefcase from the stowage compartment by Mr. Jenkins' limp feet. He hands it up to me, and when he does, I see his abdomen is soaked with blood.

I drop the case and cry out in panic. *"Help!* We need help over here!" Two flight attendants pop up from their seats now that the area is safer. I continue to scream and they rush over with a first aid kit.

"Stay with me, Dad!" I plead, taking a blanket from the overhead bin to press against the wound.

Penny places a hand on my shoulder. "Keep him still and slouched over a bit to close the wound."

"Shouldn't we lay him down?" I ask.

"NO!" Penny shakes her head firmly. "We need the wound closed and tight. Keep pressure on it." She turns her head and shouts towards the other flight attendants. "Monica, we need paramedics out here *now*."

She speaks into the interphone, and in about four minutes, paramedics come rushing in the forward door. They stride right over to Dad and get to work. One of them cuts Dad's shirt off with his trauma shears, while another dresses the wound with sterile gauze for transport to the hospital. The two EMTs lift Dad out of his seat, but then the bandage comes loose. Blood starts to flow again from the open wound.

"Jackie," Dad rasps, on the edge of consciousness. "Get that briefcase to Melinda." Then his eyes shut, and his breathing goes soft and regular.

I look at the paramedics in a panic. "Will he be okay?"

One of them nods curtly. "He'll be fine. I gave him a sedative."

Relieved, I step out of the aisle and into another row to give the paramedics more space. More first responders board the aircraft, one of them carrying a yellow spine board. Laying the board down in the aisle, the EMTs place Dad on top of the board and strap him, careful not to reopen the wound.

Once Dad is off the aircraft, I grab the briefcase he pointed out and try to leave, but I am blocked by the airport police who order me back into the cabin.

"Hi, can I help you?" I ask.

"Please step back," states a tall Caucasian man in full police gear. He looks at the corpse slumped over in the seat. "Have a seat right there." He points to row one.

"I had nothing to do with his death," I said cautiously.

"But the flight attendants told us on the ground that you tried to open the galley door in flight. That is a federal offense."

"I had to get their attention somehow," I reply.

"Ever heard of a flight attendant call button?" he howls at me. "We need to detain you for further questioning."

"What!" I yell. "You can't be serious! I saved the airliner from crashing."

He places me in handcuffs, and I start shouting. "Get Melinda Rodriguez here! She can vouch for me, and she can resolve this."

Once we reach the bottom of the stairs, I see a generous number of police cruisers and ambulances around the aircraft. He escorts me toward his own police cruiser.

Suddenly, from behind us, a male voice shouts my name. I turn around, as does the officer, and see one of the pilots waving me over.

"Ms. Jette? I want to show you something."

"Captain. She is under arrest!" He shouts back on a power trip.

The pilot, a short and stocky Latino man with a clean-shaven face, runs over to us. "You take those damn handcuffs off, now!"

"You can't tell me what to do," The officer snarled.

"This woman just saved the lives of all our passengers," the pilot shot back. "If you do not release her this instant, I, on behalf of the airline as chief pilot, will sue you and your entire department for police brutality, false arrest and whatever else our lawyers can think of. I might add that they are overpaid and always deliver."

Amused, I look up and say, "Well? I told you the truth." He ponders for a moment, frightened by the threat, he releases my wrist from the grip of the cuffs. He storms off, not bothering to say goodbye or sorry.

"Hello, Jackie. My name is Captain Roy Herald." He extends his hand for a shake. "I can't thank you enough. Because of you, my wife and children get to see me at dinner tonight."

He gives me a hug following my shake and once we break apart, he grabs my hand, and we walk over to a group of men who are standing by the number two engine with the fire department. The side doors are open on both sides of the engine.

"Why are those covers up?" I ask.

"The fan cowls are open because the mechanics wanted to see what you already knew. How you knew what would happen, I don't know. But, thank gosh you knew something."

"Not a problem," I say, trying to play it down.

"Well, that's why I wanted you to come over here before you left." He points to the number two engine.

"Bear with me, Captain. I'm not sure what exactly you are pointing at within the engine."

"No worries." He nods his head at one of the mechanics. "Ed here's got a fuel filter for this engine. I wanted to show it to you, because it's completely clogged. When we descended to a lower altitude, the fuel started leaking from the filter onto the engine, which was red hot at the time."

"And so?" I ask.

Captain Herald looks grim. "If we hadn't shut down the engine when we did, a fire was extremely likely to occur. If you hadn't intervened, we would all be dead."

"What caused it to clog, Captain?"

"We won't know until they examine the filter under a microscope, but it could be dirty fuel, ice, foreign debris — anything, really."

Before the conversation can go further, I thank him for landing us safely. "You did the hard part. Flying this creature safely onto a runway."

We turn and walk away from the engine. He leans in and makes a trembling remark. "The flight attendant said that you appeared in the last row. When they looked on the manifest just before we touched the ground, you were not listed on the flight."

Before I can respond, a black SUV pulls up by the nose of the plane. We stand silent, watching as the tires screech on the pavement. Out of it emerges a slender woman dressed in a military green shirt and green camo pants with tan boots. Her hair is covered by a green camo hat.

"Jackie Jette?" the woman shouts.

For some reason, I raise my hand to identify myself. The woman approaches the pilot and me.

"Hello, ma'am. I am Lieutenant Ashwood. I have orders to pick you up and put you on a plane right away."

I find myself frightened by this woman standing in front of me. *She must be related to Marge with that deep and powerful voice.*

"Okay." I turn and give the pilot a hug and thank him again. While we embrace, he whispers in my ear.

"Jackie, I don't know what you are or who you are, but I am grateful for the miracle you gave us today."

I tear up and walk with Lieutenant Ashwood. Once she starts up the vehicle, I'm racked with worry for my father.

"Would you please take me to the hospital where my dad is going?"

"Sorry, ma'am." She shakes her head. "My orders are to make sure you take off on that aircraft." She stops the car and points at the aircraft taking me home to Bluefin Cove.

Dejected, I thank her for driving me. But when I step into the cabin of the small jet, I'm shocked to see my father on his gurney, flanked by two paramedics. It turns out, this is a military evacuation — and Melinda's already taken care of everything.

Once I fasten my safety belt, I turn to the two paramedics. "What's the plan when we get to Maine?" I ask. "There isn't a trauma center in Bluefin, as far as I know."

"Our orders are to accompany you and this gentlemen to a trauma center about a two-hour drive from Bluefin Cove. Once he's released, we will set up a home care operation," the taller military paramedic stated.

Our flight is quick, but we make it to the Portland Memorial Air Force Base. We land, deplane into an ambulance, and head for the hospital building. Once inside, the military surgeon and nurses take Dad back.

The next three hours pass by like molasses in wintertime. I rest my head on the wall next to me as I doze off. I wake up when I feel someone tugging at my shoulder. *It's Candice.*

I am so thankful to have her here with me. "I am so happy to see you. I am going crazy down here by myself." I shout from twenty feet away.

The lady behind the desk doesn't like the loud talking and reminds me to be quiet. I quickly brush her off and run over to Candice giving her a hug and squeezing her tight, and she squeezes me too.

The next eight hours are extremely slow as we only receive an update from the volunteer desk agent. "No update, but they are doing everything they can." She says the same thing once an hour, and finally Candice tells her not to bother us until the update has changed.

After twelve straight hours, a blue-gowned man emerges from the double doors. He enters the waiting area and approaches us. I shake Candice awake, as she did me when she got here. Scared of what the doctor is going to say, I say a small prayer. "Lord, please let him live."

"Jackie?" He checks who I am before telling me the news. "Paul is resting and will be able to move in a week. He came through the surgery just fine."

"Oh, thank you, God!" I shout, and I thank the surgeon, too.

"I noticed that when we lifted his eyelid after the anesthesia wore off, his eyes were a bright white color." My heart raced. "I am going to refer you to an ophthalmic specialist to check out his eyes. In the last one hundred years of records, the military has only one other case about the white eyes. It's very rare, but I still want Paul to see the specialists."

I thank him as does Candice, and we walk back to see him. We arrive at his bedside to find him sleeping comfortably with a bandage over the now-fixed wound. We stay for a few moments, then the nurse comes in. She advises us that he will be out for a while until the anesthesia wears off, and we should go home.

There is no way that I am driving two-something hours away. Candice and I decide to get a hotel room just outside of the base. After five days living between the hotel and the base hospital, Dad is ready to go home — nearly two days early.

We make it home safely, and they get Dad all set up in his room. It's going to be a few days before he'll be up and ready to talk about what happened. *To be honest, I could use the rest. Especially after the restless stay in Portland.*

CHAPTER 16

Over the next few days, the military paramedics attend to Dad, and slowly he begins to heal and get back to his old ways. Today is Tuesday, and Candice is at her floral shop in town. Since Dad's in good hands, I grab my sweater and purse for a bike ride into town. Riding along the boardwalk, I notice the beaches are busy with tourists trying to get one last swim in before school starts in a week.

I'm sure Rita's department store is filled to the gills with back-to-school shoppers, since she's the closest clothing outlet, and she offers parents coupons if they bring in a syllabus from their children's school.

But strangely, the window displays at the floral shop are barren. That's not like Candice; she always has something proudly showcased in her windows. I park my bike outside the store and walk in to find Candice and Grace on the floor, papers scattered all around them.

"What are you guys doing?" I ask.

Candice looks up and me and laughs.

"Oh, you know. Having a very important meeting about window displays."

"Is that a wine bottle?"

Grace giggles. "Some companies order coffee. We order cheap wine and design."

"What if a customer comes in?" I ask, setting my purse on the table.

"Pfff," Candice shrugs. "We haven't had a customer today, and it's nearly 2 p.m."

I take a seat on the carpet with them. "What ideas do we have so far?"

My sister pulls a piece of construction paper from the pile and hands it to me. "So far, that's the winner!"

I review the piece of paper, then grab a marker from the floor and start to add to the drawing.

"Well, what do you gals think?" I ask, handing it back to Candice.

"Jackie, you're smart!" Candice beams. "Only... how can we make the vases look like that?"

"Grace?" I ask. "Do you have any clear cylindrical vases in the back?"

"Sure, we have a boatload!"

"Can you go grab a box, please?"

Over the next few hours, we cut out colored construction paper and printouts from the internet, fitting them inside the vases to create the illusion that the flowers are being held by giant crayons.

Then we raid the back office for school supplies, such as Scotch tape, staplers, and brightly colored markers. Candice makes a huge yellow pencil with a pink eraser out of construction paper, writing *Back to School 2023. We love our educators!* We place the sign right in the middle of the window, so the words face out toward the street.

After a few more hours of hard work and two more bottles of cheap wine, the window is bold and fun for the students, parents and teachers walking by. I guess I needed a break from reality — and so did Candice.

I ride my bike home as the sun sets and the ocean grows darker, and Candice catches a cab. When I approach our driveway, I can see she's already there.

"I win!" Candice yells from the front porch.

"Fine!" I shout back. "You win this time."

Our giggling is brought to an abrupt halt when Candice opens the door to find Dad sitting upright in the living room, the military paramedics nowhere in sight. He's watching an old movie on television, and when we walk in, he clicks it off.

"It's about time you girls got home."

CHAPTER 17

"Dad? Where are the two paramedics?" I ask.

"I sent them away," he says. "I wasn't able to fire them, so I sent them back to base. I don't need their help anymore." Candice and I join him in the living room.

By the next afternoon, Dad walks up to me while Candice is back at her shop and says that he is ready to review and talk about what happened with Mr. Jenkins on board that aircraft. I call Melinda and tell her we're ready to come into the office, and Agent Taylor picks us up the next morning at 9 a.m.

Once we arrive in Melinda's office, I see she has the briefcase I gave her when I landed back in Bluefin Cove. She tells us we're going to have a late night, since there's so much information to document and get through.

Melinda points at a file folder in front of her.

"Before we get started with Mr. Jenkins, we've had a development in the 1971 case."

She opens the folder and reveals three photos of the doomed jetliner. Dad picks up the first photo and examines it in detail.

"Where did these come from?" I ask.

"They were found on a camera that was bought at a local pawnshop in London yesterday morning. The person who bought it, a former Royal Military Commander, found the film inside and had it developed. They were sent to us by the US Embassy in London."

From what I can tell, all three photos are unremarkable exterior views of the aircraft.

"Dad, what do these photos tell you?" I ask.

Dad shuffles the photos, then arranges them on the table. "You can see that the first photo has the aircraft with the wheels retracted, but in the second photo, the wheels are halfway down and in the third and final photo, the wheels are down and locked."

"Where were these taken from?" I asked Melinda. "Do we have a location?"

Dad cuts in. "We were still over the ocean at 10,000 feet. About thirty miles out."

"So, it had to be from an ocean liner, or a cargo vessel." But something still doesn't make sense. "Wouldn't that cause immense drag on the aircraft to have the gear down that far?"

"Correct. But given that the other pilots and I didn't know the extent of the damage, we lowered the gear early to make sure it deployed correctly." Dad replied.

Dad passes me the first photo. "Look just behind the main gear," he tells me. "Do you see that?"

There's a dark spot, with some kind of black mist flowing behind it. "Is that the blast location?" I ask. Noticing that the aircraft is banked, I can see the windows spaced out. Then I begin to count the windows from the rear exit door. *Seventeen.*

"What row did we not have the files on?" I ask Melinda.

"Twenty. Row twenty."

The puzzle pieces are starting to fall into place. I pull out the Americonic 707 seat map from another file. I compare the printed seat map with the photo. The seat map displays the windows next to the seat chart. I count from the back forward. One window, two windows, and so on.

"Yep," I say. "Guess which row has the seventeenth window?"

"Row 20?" Melinda asks.

"Uh-huh."

"Dad, what's underneath the windows here and here?" I ask, pointing to the spot on the photo with my finger.

"The cargo compartment," he answers confidently. "The cargo compartment is aft of the main gear, and the fuel tanks are forward."

"Right," I say. "Now let's see who was sitting in Row 20 on this side." I open the briefcase. Inside, there are three files.

"First one." I say, grabbing the file on top. "Seat 20D. Mr. Robert Fritzel. His file is complete." I hand the file over to Melinda.

She reads the witness statement out loud. "'I was sitting in my seat, just enjoying the smooth flight, when all of a sudden, I felt the airplane descend. I knew this wasn't normal, because we had just left and were nowhere near Rome. The flight attendants were cleaning the cabin and putting items away, which was weird because they had just been setting up for dinner. While they were taking their jump seats, I heard a sort of bell sounding.' When asked to compare the sound of the alarm to an everyday alarm, the passenger said that the alarm was similar to a kitchen timer. 'The alarm sounds for a few moments, then the next thing I know, BOOM! A small hole forms where the wall meets the floor. It continues to grow bigger and bigger. It was big enough to fit a radio in. Then, things in the cabin were getting sucked out of the hole.' When asked what types of items, Robert said, 'Everything. Purses, coats, blankets and more.'"

Melinda looks up from the report. "What kind of terrorist uses a kitchen timer for a bomb?"

"Jenkins was too smart to use a kitchen timer," Dad says. "He has experience behind him. While it may have sounded like a kitchen timer, I place my bets that it was a digital timer."

Melinda nods, then opens the next file. This time she scans it and reads out just the good parts. "Seat 20E, John Townsend, said similar things in his version of the events, with one significant difference. He pointed out that the man in the seat next to him, closest to the window, was very nervous during the boarding process and was watching the ramp agents load the baggage and cargo closely. He also kept looking at his watch."

"Hmm," I muse out loud. "He must have been waiting for something to happen."

Melinda opens the last file, for seat number 20F. "You're not going to believe this," she says.

"What is it?" Dad asks.

Melinda hands over the piece of paper. "Take a look for yourself."

Dad takes it, and I lean in to read over his shoulder. There's nothing there. Just: NO COMMENT, written under the witness line.

"This must be what Mr. Jenkins was hiding from us," Melinda says. "But why?"

Dad sighs and leans back in the chair, staring at the ceiling in thought. "What is it, Dad?" I ask.

"Before departure, Mr. Jenkins brought me an envelope for my trip to Rome. When I opened it, I saw a passenger had been added at the last minute. I was to watch him in Rome, because he was carrying a special item in his luggage."

Melinda raises her eyebrows. "That's the first I'm hearing about it."

"I didn't think anything of it. I trusted Jenkins with my life for years."

"Dad, did the note say what the special item was?"

"A newly developed military device — top secret — that would change the history of time travel." Dad clears his throat, clearly uncomfortable. "I had no idea the device was a bomb that would kill me. Of course, that *did* change history. Excuse me, ladies." Flustered, he rises from his seat. "I think I need to go outside and get some air."

When he leaves, Melinda and I sit for a moment in silence. Then she startles me with her next words. "Jackie, that explains why Mr. Jenkins was so adamant about the government keeping a close eye on you."

"You're right!" I agree. "He provided me the most convenient job a person could have with good pay." Now that I think about it, he was able to keep a leash on me with the easy work and great compensation for all those years.

"But, why?" Melinda asks. "Why would he want to kill Paul, but keep an eye on you? Was he planning on killing you once you proved you could time-travel?"

Dad comes back in. We brainstorm for a while, trying to work out why Mr. Jenkins would want to kill him — the greatest asset to the United States since the atomic bomb.

Finally, Dad rises from his chair and bursts out, "I know why! I know why he wanted me dead."

Melinda and I both wait. "Why, Dad?" I ask.

He responds with two words that I never would have thought could be the answer to this bizarre case: "Candice Jette."

CHAPTER 18

"Candice?" I repeat. "What does Candice have to do with Mr. Jenkins?"

"I saved Candice from a crash when she was a baby and brought her into the future."

Melinda and I are both look at each other. "Yeaaaah…" she says. "We know that."

"But don't you see?" Dad points at the files scattered across the table. "By me bringing Candice into the future and saving her from death, what would stop the government from bringing some important person into the future — like a past president, or an admiral?"

"Why would the government want to do that?" I frown.

He smiles as if he's just cracked the code. "If you had an issue arise in the present day, say a leader is assassinated, you could send your agent to bring them into the future and therefore prevent the assassination."

"JFK?" I state, and he nods his head, telling me that is a great example.

Melinda looks stunned. "How would that work, considering you can only time travel when you touch a piece of wreckage?"

Dad smiles wickedly, like a kid who got caught sneaking a piece of candy. "Well, that's not the *entire* truth," he admits.

Melinda cocks her head to one side. "What do you mean?"

"When I started working for the government, I was afraid they would abuse my gift, maybe use it for the wrong reasons. Airplane crashes had always piqued my interest, so I decided to use my gift toward keeping air travel safer."

"Hang on," I interject. "If the government wanted to have you bring past leaders back to the present, why would Mr. Jenkins want you dead?"

Dad crosses his arms in front of his chest. "I'm not sure, but it's worth figuring out."

Melinda turns to her computer and begins typing.

"What are you doing?" I ask.

"I want to see if Mr. Jenkins received a large sum of money into his bank account recently. If he did, that would indicate a motive to have Paul and the rest of the passengers killed"

"Isn't that against the law?" I asked.

"Well, technically, yes." She stops typing and picks up a phone.

"Who are you calling?" I question her.

She ignores me. The phone rings and rings until she begins to talk. "This is Melinda Rodriguez calling for Cameron Stanton." She smiles at Dad and me. "Yes, it's Melinda. Get it all out of your system. Come on, we have work to do."

She whispers to us, placing her hand over the speaker near her mouth while the man continues to babble. "We went to college together for a year. I lost a bet *one time,* and I never get to hear the end it."

"Are you done?" Melinda snickers through the phone. "Okay, I need a warrant for a deceased suspect in Kentucky. I need to see his bank records from around the year 1971 and this year. It's urgent to national security." A long pause follows.

"He is working on it." She whispers to us. After a ten-minute hold, Melinda's computer chimes.

"Thank you, Cameron. Yes, I will make time for lunch soon," she says and hangs up the phone, returning to her computer. Cameron has sent a copy of the warrant request to her email, and now a judge needs to sign off. All we have to do now is wait.

A week later, Candice goes off to work in the early morning, giving Dad and me the house to ourselves. No plans were made to head into the office, at least not yet. Sipping coffee from my rocking chair on the porch, I enjoy the peaceful salt mist rolling off the shore and landing on my cheeks.

Dad emerges a few moments later with a sweater for me in one hand and a cup of coffee for him in the other hand. "I thought you might want your sweater." Dad smiled.

"Thank you." I say, accepting the sweater from him and bundling up while he takes a seat in the other chair. I am grateful to have this personal time with Dad. I'm going to stand my ground. Today is the day that I will find out how he time travels back.

"Dad, I want to know, and I want to know now," I say firmly. He faces me, his eyes filled with curiosity. "Tell me how you brought us home —"

He rises from his chair, trying to make a dash for the front door. I hop up strenuously, following him inside and into the kitchen.

"Dad!" I hiss. "I am not waiting for another day. You owe it to me!"

He stopped. "I owe it to you?" he glares. I stop in my tracks, filled with fear. I stay silent. "I owe you a curse? I owe you to be used and abused by the government? I owe you this curse?" We stand in a full draw, waiting for the other one to make a move.

Finally, he breaks and extends an invitation to sit at the dining table. I accept, and we both take our seats.

"Dad, I just want to know who I am, and why is it a curse?" I plead.

He shakes his head. "I have had to see hundreds of people, in the most exciting moments of their lives, with no idea that they were about to die. Christine Carter is the only person who caught me appearing in the cabin."

"You gave life to the best sister that I could have. Tears form in both of our eyes. "You made a choice, and look how grand it was."

"This is not something to be happy about," he declares. "Melinda wants you to take over and time-travel. This will eat you alive with guilt."

"I have to disagree," I answer. "On the two flights that I time-traveled to, all of the passengers landed safely. I made a choice to save them. And you are a result of my choice."

"But don't you realize that when you change history, you change the future? What changed when we came back to 2023, Jackie?"

"The airport across the way. Instead of a big open field, it's a little more sophisticated." I argue my side. "The townspeople are still the same, along with everything else. Well, and you are here."

He sighs, rising from the table to refill his coffee cup.

I continue. "Why is it so hard for you to understand that I want this? I want to help people."

"Jackie!" he hisses. "If you change the past and that aircraft does not crash, then there is no evidence box or file to travel back with. You are stuck with the future and can't change it."

"That is simply not true. We have other accidents that we can reference if I should ever have to travel back and correct something," I spit out.

"I'm afraid I don't follow."

"Should I need to go back and prevent myself from saving the people in a disaster, there are plenty of other crashes from different time periods that I can use in order to travel back."

"Jackie, that is too much work with not enough resolution," he declares. "You can rely on another crash that may have been a year or a month earlier? What will you do for a month while you wait for the aircraft you need to crash?"

I think for a moment as he does have a point. "Okay, what if," I formulate a plan, "when the plane lands safely, I take a piece of the existing aircraft with me. And when I return to our office here at Jette Industries, I file it away?"

Believing that a light bulb has illuminated, it is quickly burned out when Dad makes a rather compelling argument.

"If the plane does not crash, then there is no pain associated with the wreckage pieces. No tears are shed over those pieces and its value to you, us, and our operation is worthless. The way we can touch a piece and be sent to it last few moments are brought by the pain and suffering from those who died on board."

"Dad, you do have a point. I will admit it. But I can't let these people die. I have to try and save them." His eyes reach for the ceiling as he begins to think of a mutually agreeable solution.

After a minute in deep thought, he finally lands back in reality with me. "What if you were to save them and give them a new life with new identities? Meaning, they would still survive but not be allowed to return to their original lives."

"Then what is the point? They might as well perish on that flight." I hissed growing rather upset with him. I want to let them have a second chance at life. Not put them through this terrible ordeal and then tell them that their lives as they know it are over.

"Dad. Let's cut the bullshit," I demand, and he is taken aback. "You are being stubborn. This is going to happen whether you approve of it or not. You can either help me figure this out and save me a few painful lessons, or you can be my dad but have nothing to do with my job. The decision is yours," I say in an icy demeanor.

I do believe that I have upset him, as he storms off from the table and proceeds down the hallway towards his room. *If he is as stubborn as I am, he will be back in 3... 2...* I smile at him.

"Okay, I will help you on one condition," he offers.

I narrow my eyes and raise my brows in curiosity. "And that condition would be?"

"We have to work together on every project. I travel back with you and assess the situation. We are a team, and we work together. I will confer with you, and you will confer with me," he says. "Do we have a deal?"

Extending my arm, we shake hands, solidifying the deal. Now, I feel it is the right time to ask how he started.

Dad sighs. "This is a long story."

"We've got time," I giggle to him. The coffee is nearly empty, and before he starts, I restock the coffee pouch and brew a fresh pot.

With the coffee brewed, I top off his mug and retake my seat at the table. He begins his story with my first question. "How old were you when you figured out that you have a gift?"

"The first time was my twenty-second birthday. I had just received my pilot's license to fly crop sprayers — those are small one-person aircraft that fly over fields to fertilize the plants — and I was taking the aircraft for a little joyride after I ran out of fluid. While flying over a vacant field, I saw the remnants of a World War II plane. I wasn't sure what type, but my curiosity got the better of me and I landed in the open field after completing one pass over to inspect the landing surface."

He takes a break to sip his coffee. "I stumbled around until I discovered that the field is an abandoned World War II base. The large barn turned out to be a hangar filled with relics of the past. Airplane parts loitered the interior shelves and walls.

"The artifacts were fascinating and covered in dust. I must have emptied a dozen boxes and the thirteenth box was the one that would change my life and now yours too. The outside of the box was labeled *Brewster F2A Buffalo testing aircraft*. I lifted the lid and saw a bunch of broken gauges and pieces of metal. I carefully picked up the joystick which was snapped in half."

I lean in, waiting for the rest of the story. He takes another sip of coffee and continues.

"Suddenly, I was sitting inside of the empty aircraft in 1942 at that same air base. Only, the base was staffed. When a soldier noticed my presence, he rushed right over and began yelling at me, demanding that I exit the aircraft post haste. I rushed out of the plane and back onto the tarmac, where this slightly large man grabs my shirt collar and lifts it up."

Dad chuckles for a moment. I bet he wasn't laughing when it was happening.

"He asked if I was a Nazi spy. I couldn't help but laugh at the idea, considering when I left, it was 1960. After I failed to convince him that I wasn't a spy, he locked me up in the office. The office was tiny and more of a storage closet, but it had me scared."

"So, what did you do?" I ask. "How did you get out of it?" I can barely contain my excitement for his answer.

"I closed my eyes and prayed. When that didn't work, I thought about the day I left. I focused hard on the day that I left, May 20. I felt my eyes twitch — which was the first time that had happened. Then suddenly, I woke up on the opposite end of the field. I had to walk quite a distance to reach my airplane. I couldn't fire that plane up fast enough and get home."

"What happened when you got home and had time to think about it?" I asked.

Adjusting himself in the wooden chair, he repositioned his stance.

"The only person that I could trust with this information and not to lock me in the insane asylum was your great-grandmother, Margaret. I felt like such an idiot telling her, but when I finished, she went into her bedroom. I speculated that she was either calling my parents or the doctors." He paused again to polish off the last drop of coffee in his mug.

"She emerged with a black journal-like book and sat next to me on the couch. Before she opened the book, she gave me a hug and a kiss on the cheek, telling me everything is going to be okay. Suspicious, I asked how she knew that. Her reply was something that I never could have imagined. I can still remember her words to this day. Every single one of them.

"*Paulie, when I turned 32, I was on a train with your grandfather heading from Dallas to New York. We went to a business meeting in Dallas for his company and while on the train, I stumbled on a cargo car instead of the dining car. There were boxes stacked to the ceiling, and one in particular grabbed my attention. It was labeled Dallas Flyer Investigation. Curious, I opened the box and found some files and a piece of the train. A lever, I think. When I picked up the lever, I was suddenly on the train. Once I figured out the train that I was on was the Dallas Flyer, I pulled the emergency brake, stopping the train before it collided with a disabled freight train on the same track.* She did the same thing I did, and focused on the date she left. When she reappeared in the present day, she had to explain via long-distance telephone why she was in Tulsa, four miles from a train depot. How she sold grandpa on that, I have no idea."

I whipped out my telephone and researched the Dallas Flyer. Reading up on the story, I couldn't believe how she saved the lives of 200 passengers, just like I did with the two aircraft landing safely. I can't help but wonder what color my eyes will be.

My thought is interrupted when I hear a knock at the door. *Who can that be? It's only 10 a.m.* I head over to the door and see a man standing behind the sheer window curtain. As I move closer to the window, I can see it is Agent Taylor.

Unlocking the door, I swing it open and welcome him inside.

"Melinda sent me over to pick you and Paul up," he says. "She got a response about the warrant and needs us there."

I head into the kitchen and tell Dad. I grab my purse following dad out of the house and down to Agent Taylor's car.

CHAPTER 19

"After seven days, Cameron was able to get an expedited approval by a judge in Kentucky," Melinda said as we stood around her desk. Filled with abundant excitement, we proceeded with the search for Mr. Jenkins's bank records, starting with his name.

"You should check around the time of the 1971 flight, too," I tell her.

But after a few minutes of searching the databases and a quick phone call to Melinda's friend at the FBI, Mr. Jenkins comes up clean. Dad asks Melinda to look up his wife Suzie Jenkins, and again, her name is clean. Nothing but routine payments from legitimate companies.

Melinda searches for every type of payment transaction that her computer will allow. Just when I've about given up, I hurry over to the briefcase and inspect it more closely.

"Do you have a black light?" I ask Melinda.

Melinda locates one in the bottom rear drawer of her desk. She hands it to me, and I tell Dad to hit the lights.

With the lights out, I scan the briefcase for oily fingerprints, but the case is covered in fingerprints. Getting creative, I start to scan the pockets on the inside. Still, I have no luck. I ponder for a moment. Dad flips the switch, and the lights illuminate.

Aunt Jess would always think outside of the box. I feel the lining of the case with my fingertips, completing a full interior search. Arriving at the last corner, I feel a hole in the fabric. Inserting my nail, the fabric fails back.

"Ahh, found it!" I pull back the briefcase lining, revealing a 4x6 size piece of paper.

"Hot damn!" I shout, turning over the scrap paper. "It's a bank receipt from a bank in Sweden."

"Let me see it, please," Melinda says, and I hand it to her. She scans the document and stops at the numbers printed at the bottom of the receipt. Navigating her way back to the computer, she begins typing the numbers into her computer search browser and says, "Bingo!"

"What did you find?" I ask.

"This routing number is not for a bank in Sweden, but for a small-town bank in Sweden, Kentucky," Melinda states.

"Where in the hell is Sweden, Kentucky?" Dad asks.

I haven't heard of it either. So, I look it up in the navigation app on my phone.

"Sweden is two hours east of Louisville," I say. "How much was the amount for?" Melinda's jaw lowers. "Is it a lot?"

"Mhmm," she purses her lips together. "5.2 million dollars is the account balance." We all lower our mouths in astonishment. The fact that someone paid this man over five million dollars to kill Dad and the passengers throws everyone for a loop.

Finding the courage to speak first, Dad says, "Does it say the name on the bank account?"

"Yes, it does," she replies without the need for a speech assistant. "Jane Damhirschkuh.

is the name on the receipt."

"How did you pronounce that so well?" I ask her, amazed.

Melinda giggles. "I majored in German while attending Columbia University."

"Do you know what it means?" Dad inquires, as the name is very unique.

"No, I don't," she answers. "But I am sure that a Google search can assist us." Melinda returns to the computer, typing in the search bar. After a few seconds, her mouth lowers.

"What is it?" I ask her.

"The word literally means Doe. The name on the account is Jane Doe." We all chuckle for just a moment. The irony is grand. A secret account in the name of Jane Doe. There is no way to look that up in the system, as a multitude of results will populate.

I am not a detective, but if I had to bet, I would place a high wager on the bank security cameras. With the search warrant approved, we should be able to contact the bank and review who last touched the account. Advising Melinda of my idea, we formulate the plan and have Cameron contact the bank's legal department. This way, everything will be through proper channels. The money had to go somewhere.

Cameron contacts Melinda via email a day later. The legal department at Sweden National Bank was very helpful. Cameron sent over our request to see the matching security camera video for every moment that the account was accessed in person.

The days drag on and we get no response from Cameron. After two weeks, Melinda finally receives a response from Cameron, and it's not to our liking.

"What do you mean the bank burned down?" I thunder.

"Old wiring, according to the fire inspector," Melinda sighs.

"What do we do now?" Dad asks.

Not sure how to proceed, we all pitch ideas, but none of them make it off of the ground. The spinning office chairs work overtime, and we all stare off into space trying to think of another way to see who accessed the account.

"Melinda!" I boom. "Are there any businesses across the street that have security cameras?" With her attention and Dad's on me, I continue. "Cameron sent over the digital logs from the account, so we know days and times. Can we use a neighboring business to check security cameras?"

Jumping at the idea, we head for Sweden. Only for this destination, I don't need my passport. I send Candice a text to let her know not to wait up for us. After a quick two in a half hour flight to the airport near Sweden, Agent Taylor sets up a private hire car, and it takes us to the small town.

Cornfields surround the town, along with a large red barn here and there. The cornstalks sway in the wind as the breeze rolls over the plains. I expect a tornado at any moment with the thunderstorms building in the distance.

One second, we're cruising down the road at 75 miles an hour, then we're in a small town. Before we enter the main street, we are greeted by a large blue sign with green lattice that reads *Welcome to Sweden, Population 7470.*

The buildings on Main Street — the only street — are something out of a western movie. I expect to see a stagecoach arriving beside us. There are a few old cars roaming the parking spots in front of businesses with boarded-up windows.

We pull up to what is left of the bank. A pile of charred rubble is all that remains. Funny, the bank vault is still standing considering it is made of concrete and steel. Standing around the mess, I look around for any security cameras, but nothing sticks out. I thought Bluefin Cove was outdated. Boy, was I wrong.

"Agent Taylor, I don't see any cameras here," I say.

He looks at me, then around the street. The only buildings that surround the bank are vacant with large LEASE HERE signage in the windows. Agent Taylor and I walk across the street, searching for any storefronts that may have a camera. We walk up and down the street without any hope.

While we stand on the street corner in front of the bank after our exhaustive search, I witness the reddest cardinal fly over us and complete a coordinated landing on the second-floor balcony across the street. The store below is a bookshop with an open sign flashing in the window. My eyes are transfixed on the bird resting its feet on the iron fencing, until my eyes navigate to the left and see a wildlife camera bolted to the fence post. I look back at the bank and then back to the bird.

"What is it, Jackie?" Agent Taylor asks while Dad and Melinda are focusing on the ashy rubble.

As I point up to the bird and the camera beside it, Agent Taylor's head follows.

"See that bird?" He nods. "There is a wildlife camera right next to it."

"So?" he mumbles. "Do you want a close-up of the bird?"

I giggle at his remark. "No, but those wildlife cameras have excellent picture-taking capability. Look at the way it is pointed down." I let him assess the angle of the camera. "It's pointed right at the bank. Any motion would make the camera click a picture."

"We need to find out who owns that camera," Melinda blurts out from behind us. I had no idea that she and Dad had walked up behind us. All four of us walk across the street and around the building to find an entrance or a lobby that leads upstairs, but the building is walled all the way around except for the front door, which enters the bookshop.

"I am going to run inside and see if the employee knows who lives up there," I say and enter the bookshop.

Shelves line the inner walls, and there are two islands in the middle containing a majority clearance books, new editions and best sellers. The store is dusty with a few cobwebs lurking in the corners.

"Hello, welcome to Books of Sweden. Can I help you find a particular book?" a sweet older lady in her seventies says from behind the counter with her rich Kentucky accent. I walk up her to and introduce myself.

"Well, I am not looking for a book today. I need to find who lives in the apartment upstairs," I declare.

"Who wants to know?" the lady asked. By this time, I had noticed the name tag pinned to her blouse.

"Gwen, I am investigating a criminal who tried to hijack a NorthJet flight in Louisville about a week ago." Her eyes grow wide with excitement and suspicion. "Before we could see the bank's security camera footage, it burned down."

"I told Mr. Hollings to fix the wiring years ago," she jumps in before taking a drink out of her coffee cup. "It's a shame that the old building burned down. My dear friend, Suzie Jenkins, worked at that bank for thirty years before she died last winter."

"I am so sorry to hear of her passing." I said as I don't recall ever hearing that name before. "Gwen, does your camera always record when birds fly in front of it?"

"Mhmm." She nods. "Do you want to see some of the photos?"

"Do you know the person who lives there? I don't want to intrude."

"You're looking at her," she says, grabbing the keys, and we walk through the rear of the shop where a hidden staircase is situated to the left. Up the stairs and into a small hallway, we reach the glass door leading to the porch. Once on the porch, she pops the camera open and retrieves a small memory card from the slot. "Is this what you need, dear?"

"Yes ma'am." I reach for the card and accept it from her. "How old is this card?"

"It has been in there for a month or so," she says and then starts to walk back inside. I follow, and we return to her counter in the store where she pulls out a calendar. Flipping back to the previous month, she points to a date circled in red marker at the beginning of July. "I thought so. I changed the memory card on July 3. So, I am due to change it."

"I will give you this back before I leave today," I say and leave the shop with her sitting back at the desk.

I walk out and regroup with everyone. Providing the card to Agent Taylor, he returns to the car and pulls out his bulky laptop, putting it on the hood, which I don't think made the driver too happy. With it powered up, he inserts the card and uploads the pictures.

The humidity is absolutely terrible today and I feel my back slick with sweat. "Agent Taylor? I believe that we would be more comfortable inside of the car where the air conditioning is?" I phrase it as a question, but it is really a statement. Melinda seconds the idea and, in a few seconds, we are inside the car cooling off.

We watch over his shoulders as he navigates the pictures. Melinda pulls up the list on her phone of time stamps when the account was accessed. "The last one was a day before the fire. Tuesday, August 8 at 11:04 a.m."

Agent Taylor scrolls down the photos, reading the timestamps. He arrives at the date to see a few photos, most of them with birds. Until he sees a particular three-second video. We watch, trying to figure out who is walking from the street out of view into the bank.

The character is a little blurry, but Agent Taylor zooms in on the image.

"Okay, I see a figure with white hair, in a sweater, wearing heels and carrying a small brown purse with beaded handles," he says.

"That could be anyone!" Melinda hisses. "What about an exit photo? Anything when the figure emerged from the bank heading towards the camera?"

He backs out and scrolls again. Ten minutes later, the same figure is caught leaving the bank. "Look at that!" Dad points to the image. "The figure is looking right at the camera as if they know that it's there."

I couldn't tell who the figure was by the rear photo but with the front photo, there is no doubt that the figure is Gwen. Gwen is the person making the deposit.

"Why would the bookstore owner be making such a large bank transaction?" I wonder.

"You know who this is?" Melinda speaks up.

"Yes, she is the one who owns the shop and the camera," I respond.

"That is why she looked at the camera. It's hers," Dad spat from the rear seat.

"But, why would she have anything to do with the account?" Melinda questions as if I know the answers.

"The only reason that I can think for her to be there is to bank herself or to see a friend."

"Friend?" Agent Taylor spits.

"Well, while I was in her shop, she mentioned a friend who passed recently and maybe she was seeing other friends who worked inside of the bank? Given that this a small town."

"What was the friends name, Jackie?" Melinda asks.

"Suzie Jenkins." I sound out slowly trying to remember the name. "Her friend for over thirty years."

"Wait, Suzie Jenkins?" Dad asks. "That is Mr. Jenkins wife. She runs the crew check-in desk at the airport in New York."

Melinda jumps in the conversation and wants to head inside to ask more questions. I stop the idea, as Gwen is a sweet lady who will feel ganged up on. "Let me go. Just me. I don't want her to feel scared."

"Okay, but I need you to ask how and why she was touching the account," Melinda commands. Agent Taylor removes the memory card from the slot once the photos have downloaded and hands it to me.

I exit the private car, letting the humidity hit my face once again.

"Hello again, Gwen," I shout closing the door behind me. I walk up to her counter and see her still sitting in the same spot.

She looks on the countertop where a small antique clock sits. "Are you already finished? That wasn't even thirty minutes."

"Yes, technology is so fast now. I found what I was looking for, and here is your card back." I hand it to her. "I made sure not to mess with the wildlife photos either." There are two chairs nestled in between the two islands of books, and I invite Gwen to sit with me.

"It has been so long since someone has asked me to sit here. Suzie was the last person, nearly nine months ago," Gwen points out with a tear in her eye.

"Gwen, I reviewed the photos, and according to the time stamp on the bank account and the photo, you are the one who emptied the bank account just before the fire."

Offend by my accusation, she denies having anything to do with a criminal. "I had nothing to do with a criminal or the bank burning down."

"The photo suggests otherwise. What were you doing there at the exact same time?" I asked her.

"The day before it burned down?" She thinks for a moment looking up at the ceiling, then down to a photo on the end table between us. I see there is a colorized photo of two women. I suspect that the photo is her and Suzie.

"Is that Suzie?" I say, picking up the 4x6 photo frame.

"Yes, that was taken on a trip to New York in 1988. A few days before the fire, I received a letter from Suzie's granddaughter in Germany. I was listed on the college account as a secondary when Suzie became so ill. Her ex-husband still lives in New York. When she sent me a letter asking for assistance with her account, I would either walk across the street and deposit a check or get a cashier's check in the amount she needed for her schooling and mail it to her."

"Let me guess, Jane Damhirschkuh?" I ask. Her eyes enlarge with alarm when I say the correct name on an account when she didn't tell me who the granddaughter was. "Where did you send the cashier's check?"

"I put it in the mailbox, like I always do." She points to the mailbox by the front entrance. It was picked up the next day." Gwen rises from her chair and returns behind the counter in search of something.

"What are you searching for?" I ask from my chair.

"I have the original letter with the return address." She whips out a piece of paper, and I join her at the desk. She lays out the letter and the envelope in which it had arrived.

I examine the letter, and I suspect it is typed on an old typewriter based on the way the letters are not evenly printed on the paper. The letter E is lower than the rest of the letters.

"This is great. May I have these?" I ask.

"Sure, I closed the account per the letter's instruction. I don't need them anymore." She jabbers. "Be sure to send me a letter down the road."

"I sure will!" I confide and give her a hug. "Thank you for helping me. I will send you a postcard from Bluefin Cove as soon as I get home."

"Where is Bluefin Cove?" She asked.

"I said the same thing about Sweden. Bluefin is up in Maine." I wave one last time to her. "Goodbye, Gwen." She waves back, and I exit the shop, hopping back into the private car.

"So?" Melinda spats.

"Here is a letter and a return address where Gwen sent the cashier's check. It's to Suzie's granddaughter who is going to college in Germany," I say sarcastically.

"Granddaughter, really? Mr. Jenkins was unable to have children." Dad chuckled. "Furthermore, Suzie never wanted kids. She had a plane full of nieces and nephews to entertain."

"Someone conned an old lady, Dad. The nicest lady in town, too," I pointed out.

Melinda reviews the letter, reading it. "Wow, this is on a typewriter. I haven't seen a letter typed on one of those in years. Funny, it drops the letter e."

Dad snatches the letter from her hand and looks at it. "Excuse me! I was reading that." Melinda fussed at him, but he ignored her words.

"Dad?" I called. "Dad?"

"It's no coincidence that this typewriter drops the same letter as a typewriter used by an agent in the Berlin office."

"Mr. Jenkins wasn't the only agent or handler you had?" Melinda asked.

"He would have me fly through Berlin a few times a year to receive secret paperwork for the Department of Defense." He paused for a moment and looked used. "Now that I think about it, Jenkins would give me an envelope, and I would pass it on to the agent in Berlin at our base there and vice versa on the way back to the States."

"What were inside of the envelopes?" Melinda inquired.

"I don't know. I never opened them, thinking they were for the DoD."

"Who is this agent?" she asked. "He has to be dead by now or close to it."

Our conversation is interrupted when Melinda's phone rings.

"Hello, Sally, I'm in the middle of something right now." Melinda pauses to let Sally speak, and we all watched as her jaw lowers. "We are on our way to the jet. I am sending you armed guards to watch the exterior of the building. You give him anything he wants to hold him there." Melinda hangs up.

"Agent Taylor, I need a dozen armed guards at our building now. Who can we get?"

He picks up his phone from the car beverage holder and says, "We can get the Coast Guard there quicker, since they are on site." Melinda nods in agreement. "I will call them now," he says.

"This is Agent Taylor from Jette Industries. I need twelve guards to secure the perimeter of our building, now. We are heading for the airport and should be there within two hours."

Once he hangs up, he calls someone else. "Captain, this is Agent Taylor. We are heading for the airport now. Please add as much fuel as you can take on the aircraft. We need to return to Maine at the max speed the plane can handle." He pauses. "I don't care about the cost. Fill it up." He hangs up.

Dad and I turn towards each other. Our eyes make contact in the confusion about what is going on.

"Melinda, what is happening." I ask.

"Paul, the agent's name is not Conrad Schneider, is it?" Dad nods, puzzled about her guess. "Well, guess who just walked into the lobby at the airport asking to speak with me by name?"

"No way!" I shout.

"Mhmm," she responds. "He is sitting in my office with Sally right now."

"Hence the guards?" Dad chuckles.

She confirms, as she wants no one to leave the building or enter it. We hurry down the road as the private driver speeds over the speed limit. Agent Taylor slipped him a hundred-dollar bill to floor it.

The aircraft is waiting for us, and the fuel truck has just driven away when we pull up. As we settle in the seats, the pilot comes back and confirms with Agent Taylor and the massive fuel bump he requested. He hands him an invoice from the fueler, and Agent Taylor adds it to his briefcase. We make it back to the airport in Maine in one hour and forty-nine minutes.

The armed guards are holding their posts when we step off the aircraft in front of the offices. We head into the building and straight into Melinda's office, where the gentleman awaits.

CHAPTER 20

"Hello Mr. Schneider," Melinda extends her hand to shake his before taking a seat. Agent Taylor, Dad and I are sitting in the back of the room.

The older man, who must be in his eighties, sits there with his head held high. His hair is all white and cut tight. Although his eyes are bright blue, the wrinkles in his face show his true age. He wears a light blue sweater with dark blue trousers. He looks as if he just hopped off of the nursing home shuttle to shop at the market.

"How can I help you, Mr. Schneider?" she asks the frail gentleman.

He turns around and waves to Paul.

"You haven't changed a day since I last saw you in April 1971. Good for you," he says. His voice hardly has an accent as his English is near perfect.

Returning his attention to Melinda, he answers her question. "I have terminal brain cancer. I want to enter heaven without a diversion to a fiery damnation. I have flown all this way to tell you —."

Melinda cuts him off. "What does that have to do with us?"

Upset by how rudely she had cut him off, he gathers his thoughts and responds firmly.

"This has nothing to do with you or this luxury building. I am here to make amends with Paul before I die."

Dad rises from his seat and approaches the man.

"Dad, don't do anything rash," I say.

He sits down in the chair next to his former friend. "I can forgive you, Conrad. But you have to tell us why. I need to know why," he pleads.

Conrad takes a moment to catch his breath and begins to explain why.

"In 1971, I received a wire from Mr. Jenkins about a way to make a whole lot of money via a large sale. Worth millions. My greed overcame my morals. I was intrigued with his idea, and we met the following week to discuss the idea."

Dad interrupts. "That is why he flew on my flight to Berlin in April of 1971."

"Correct," Conrad confirms. "We had dinner and discussed a way to kidnap you and sell you to the highest bidder. The idea that any powerful government could bring a past leader into the present and rule with an iron fist would bring us millions, maybe more. Especially in Germany. We could bring back Adolf Hitler to rule once again."

"Why would you want him back?" I chime in, unable to keep my mouth shut.

"We were once a superpower, and we needed to be one again," he answers. "We could bring Hitler back as a new leader with a different name. He could learn from the past mistakes and progress us forward as a stronger nation."

"What was the plan officially between Jenkins and you?" Agent Taylor questions.

"The plan was to send Paul to Berlin on a special assignment under the pretense of investigating a Boeing 727 cargo crash that happened in November of 1966. Mr. Jenkins would accompany him over, and once we were off the airport grounds, Paul would be arrested by federal police officers — who we had paid a great sum of money — and taken to a secure facility. We would then have you placed on the black market as a time-travel asset with documentation to prove it after purchase."

"You do know that I am a time traveler!" Dad laughs. "I could have time-traveled into the past and created a plan to stop this."

"We had a plan for that," Conrad responds. "Once the sale was complete and the money was in our hands — or in our multiple suitcases

— you would be shot and your family would be neutralized as well. This way, we could insure our future and not have any troubles."

"So, if you needed Paul alive, why did Mr. Jenkins sabotage the Americonic flight?" Melinda inquires.

"That was an accident," he says sadly.

"How!" Dad spits. "The device was loaded in the cargo hold and Mr. Jenkins put it there."

Nodding his head, Conrad agrees. "The device loaded in the cargo hold was for your demise here in Berlin. It was supposed to be on your flight to Berlin the following week but was sent earlier due to a clerical error at the base or with Mr. Jenkins's office. I'm not sure which."

"So, the people on my aircraft would have been just collateral damage!" Dad shouts at him.

"If Paul's plane never crashed, how did you know that it was the cause of the chaos?" Melinda chimes in.

"Jenkins called me in Berlin after news broke of the disappearance. He advised me that paperwork showed his shipment was sent earlier than assigned. Mishandling by the loading agents must have switched the timer on. When the plane burned down to dust and no body was found, Jenkins and I put a new plan in to operation."

"Keep an eye on me," I say in a grim tone.

He nods. "Yes, Mr. Jenkins sent the check to your mother for her to start over. I found Bluefin Cove on a map by just finger picking a state and placing my index finger on one random spot. My nail landed on a small town in Maine, and then we sent your mother a bunch of advertisements that I had crafted about the town. It was to our benefit that the town's mayor was selling his house for a bargain price. Beverly could buy the house and have money left over."

He pauses, wetting his lips.

"Mr. Jenkins placed special agents posing as beach-going tourists to keep an eye on you. How do you think we found out about you losing your job? An agent overheard your telling Ruby about it over a cup of coffee, and if I can remember correctly, an order of pumpkin cinnamon pancakes."

My eyes grow wide as I realize that his credibility has just become rock solid. He continues. "When the agent observed you wishing for a work-from-home job for data entry, Mr. Jenkins and I conspired to create the fake law firm and therefore the fake job. We set the plan in motion and watched you closely. The file boxes were bugged with tiny microphones. We heard everything when Agent Taylor came over that day."

Melinda turns to Agent Taylor. "Didn't you sweep the house!" she spits at him.

"It is not his fault, Melinda. I had the file boxes by the front door. He did sweep the pictures, lamps and the bookshelf," I chime in.

Conrad — who had begun to cough — continues on. "When Mr. Jenkins called to advise me that our plan was in the works, I told him I was too old and had no interest in hurting anyone. I stood my ground with him from Berlin. When he found out that Jackie had time-traveled back to 1971, he called around looking for the highest bidder."

"Why wait all of these years to find out?" I ask him.

"He did not want to jump the gun and get you hurt before he could get his fortune," he sighs.

"Why was he going to Sweden, Kentucky?" Melinda demands.

"We had sold Jackie to the German government for 5.2 million US dollars. Jenkins was headed for Sweden with the only proof —"

"The paper bank receipt that Gwen had deposited," I interrupt him.

"Mhmm," Conrad confirms.

"Where did the money go?" Melinda asks, pulling out the torn envelope from Gwen. "The return address says New York."

"I retrieved the envelope at a post office box in New York. I sent her a letter pretending to be Jane Damhirschkuh to close the account once I heard that Jenkins was dead. She is a sweet lady from what I've heard. Sure enough, the cashier's check arrived in New York soon after I flew over from Berlin."

"What did you do with the money?" Melinda asks again.

"I sent the money over to the German government with a note to cancel the transaction for Operation Power Travel. The check should be arriving there anytime." Conrad pauses for a moment. "Can I have a glass of water?"

Agent Taylor walks over to the water fountain and retrieves him a cup. "Here." He musters and retakes his seat. Conrad opens a pill bottle, places a pill in his mouth, and swallows it down.

"Why did the bank burn? Did an agent orchestrate that too?" I ask once he has gulped the water down.

"That was just luck. Old ass building in a flyover town? I couldn't have planned that better," he giggles and begins to breathe more heavily. "I hope that my coming here brings you peace of mind, and that this is over. Mr. Jenkins and I are the only ones who knew outside of this office."

He turns to me, sweat now forming on his forehead.

"Conrad, are you okay?"

Ignoring my concern, he slurs his words to me, not making sense.

"Jackie, please perform your gift to the moon."

He falls to the floor, coughing and gasping for air. Looking closer, I notice a small amount of white foam coming from the corner of his mouth.

"Something's wrong!" I scream and fall to my knees. I turn him over, believing that he is choking, while the other three stay in their seats and watch. "He's choking! Don't just sit there!"

"Jackie, stop," Melinda says with no remorse in her voice. "He took a pill filled with poison to release him from suffering in the US prison system."

"You knew?" I say to her while he convulses in my arms.

"Not at first. The thought did cross my mind when he was spilling his guts to us. A top-secret agent, who is working both sides, would never confess this magnitude of information to the enemy without knowing the consequences he would endure."

"I concur," Agent Taylor says, and Dad nods. "When he swallowed the pill, I timed the reaction with the clock on her desk. Exactly two minutes from swallow, just as designed by the military. The CIA and other artificial intelligence agencies have a similar escape route."

Conrad convulses one final time, with more white foam rising from his mouth. Then he smiles slightly as his eyes float to the ceiling. Freedom takes over his body, and then he is dead.

I move back to my chair but I never remove my eyes from the corpse. I sit there just staring at him. *Wham!* I feel a slap on my shoulder that is bound to leave a bruise.

"Snap out of it!" Melinda shouts at me. I had no idea that she moved from her chair.

Shaken by death, I finally respond. "I'm sorry. That is the first time that someone has killed themselves in front of me."

Melinda pulls the chair away from the corpse and sits directly in front of me, grabbing both of my hands with hers.

"Jackie, I know this was difficult for you, but you have to pull yourself together." I agree, and she returns to her desk.

"What did we see here?" Melinda directs the questions to all of us.

Agent Taylor is the first to answer and I am glad, because I have no idea what to say. "We all witnessed a man confess a lifetime of crime and commit suicide."

"But that is what happened," I spit out in honest ignorance.

"Just wanted to make sure that we were all on the same page," she notes. "Now, before his death, he gave us the answers that we needed."

"All of this was for money and greed?" Dad says. "They were willing to kill a hundred people for money."

He looks over to me. "Jackie, thank you for saving my life, my passengers' lives and for letting me get to know you and Candice." A tear crawls down his cheek. "It has been a pleasure to meet you both as well," he says, focusing on Melinda and Agent Taylor.

"What do we do now?" I ask the team.

"Well, I have a lot of documenting to take care of in order to close this case. I could not be prouder of you both for taking the risk to solve this mystery," Melinda says.

Agent Taylor drives us home in the dark, his Tesla gliding over the wet road as rain batters the windows. The porch lights on our house are still illuminated, and I can see Candice watching us from the window.

Dad and I thank Agent Taylor, and he speeds off to the end of the street where his house is. Candice opens the front door and gives us each a hug. The rain that had once stopped begins again and bolts of lightning light up the sky around us.

"How long has it been storming, Candice?" I ask, hanging my purse on the rack.

"Oh, I closed the shop at four and the sky was beginning to sprinkle down." She looks out of the front window and then down at her watch. "So, about six hours."

"There is another storm heading for us, according to the weather program." Dad says, sitting on the couch and still calling everything on TV *a program.*

"So, where have you guys been?" Candice grins. Dad and I look at each other, not saying a word. "Come on! Tell me, I bet it was exciting."

"Oh, it was something, all right," I say, heading for the kitchen.

"Dad? Can you tell me what happened?" Candice begs. I feel bad, as she is the outsider in this mess but also the main reason. Had Dad never saved her, he would have been able to live out his life with Mom and me.

When he brought her to the future, he created a way for greedy evil men to make a buck and kill anyone to get away with it.

On the other hand, if had Dad not saved her, I would not have the best sister a person could hope for. I am glad that the two men responsible for all of this chaos are dead. Dad decides to tell Candice everything. We sit at the table until the sun rises, drinking a mixture of hot tea and coffee. The coffee was for Dad. Candice and I had the hot tea.

As the sunlight peeks through the broken clouds of the late-night storm, we rise from the table and head to our rooms. Before I can crawl into bed, I take a long steaming shower. That always gets me in a sleep mood.

Now, dressed in my coziest pajamas, I whip the covers back, excited to see my bed. Under the covers, I feel warm and safe. Reaching out to switch off my table lamp, I nearly knock over my water glass.

When I wake up twelve hours later, I see a missed call from Agent Taylor. I didn't realize that my ringer was off, but I apparently needed the rest. By swiping the screen, I unlock the phone to see a voicemail from him.

"Jackie, this is Agent Taylor. While the case of your dad's flight is closed, Melinda has learned of a new development. When the military doctors researched the white eyes displayed by your father during his emergency surgery, they found one matching case from 1985. According to medical records and DNA tests, the matching person is your brother."

The phone slips from my hand and smacks the rug at my bedside. *Did he really just say brother?*